THE SECRET IN THE OLD ATTIC

Nancy Drew races against time to unravel the clues in a dead man's letters. If she succeeds, Philip March and his little granddaughter can be saved from financial ruin. Following the obscure clues, Nancy undertakes a search for some unpublished musical manuscripts which she believes are hidden in the dark, cluttered attic of the rundown March mansion. But someone else wants them enough to put many frightening obstacles in Nancy's way.

It takes courage and ingenuity for the alert young detective to discover the significance of the skeleton with the upraised arm and to find the source of the spooky sounds of music in the old attic.

Startling developments await Nancy when she aids her lawyer father in doing some detective work on a case involving a stolen formula for a unique silk-making process. How she outwits a trio of ruthless thieves and solves the Marches' problems as well as her father's case makes exciting reading.

"You've uncovered a clue, Susan!" Nancy exclaimed

The Secret
in the
Old Attic

BY CAROLYN KEENE

GROSSET & DUNLAP
Publishers • New York
A member of The Putnam & Grosset Group

Acknowledgement is made to Mildred Wirt Benson, who under the pen name
Carolyn Keene, wrote the original NANCY DREW books

8 9 10

Contents

The Secret
in the
Old Attic

CHAPTER I

A Challenge

"IT seems strange to hunt for a clue among these, Nancy, but that's exactly what I've been asked to do."

Carson Drew was gazing at a pack of letters tied with blue ribbon, which he had taken from his pocket. He laid them on the dining-room table.

He was the outstanding attorney of River Heights and had won many difficult cases by his brilliant, clear thinking.

"What's the clue about?" Nancy asked.

"Some lost music."

"Music? What kind?"

"Popular songs, I believe, which haven't been published yet," Mr. Drew replied. "This task isn't exactly to my liking. I understand these are love letters, and—"

Nancy smiled as he rather clumsily tried to

1

loosen the knot in the ribbon that bound the letters. She offered to do it for him, and he looked relieved.

"Please tell me more about the case," she begged. "Maybe I can help you with it."

"I believe you can," her father replied, his eyes twinkling. "I'd say this is more your kind of mystery than mine, Nancy."

He looked affectionately at the slim, blue-eyed girl. Mr. Drew was proud of his eighteen-year-old daughter, who had gained a reputation of her own by solving many mysteries. She and her father had been very close since the death of Mrs. Drew when Nancy was only three, and had come to depend on each other for advice and assistance.

"What are you supposed to look for in these letters?" Nancy asked.

"I don't know," her father replied. "The instructions were vague. This afternoon, while I was away from my office, an elderly man named Philip March left the letters with my secretary. He asked that I look through them for a clue as to where certain original songs that have disappeared might have gone."

"Who composed them?" asked Nancy.

"I don't know."

Nancy had untied the ribbon, and now handed the letters to her father. He pulled one from its envelope and read it hastily.

"This is your kind of mystery, Nancy," said Mr. Drew

"I don't find any clue here," the lawyer said a few moments later. "Read this, Nancy, and see what you make of it."

The letter had been written four years ago by a young lieutenant named Fipp to his wife Connie.

"I don't see any clue, either," Nancy said. "Do you suppose Fipp is a nickname for Philip, and he's Mr. March's son?"

"Probably," Mr. Drew agreed, handing the other letters to his daughter. "I'm mighty embarrassed going through these. Love letters never were meant to be read by the outside world."

Nancy respected her father's opinion. Yet she felt that if Mr. March was a close relative of the writer, he would not have shown the letters to anyone without a very good reason.

"Have you ever met Mr. March?" she asked.

"I think not. But he may be a member of a family that lived on an estate up the river a few miles. Well, we'll soon know about the letters. Mr. March is coming here this evening."

Nancy was eager to meet him. While waiting, she read the letters, pausing at several lovely verses in them. Nowhere, however, could she find any clue to lost or hidden music.

"Do you suppose these verses are the words of the songs?" she mused. "Maybe they're—"

Just then the bell rang and Nancy hurried to the door. The caller was a gray-haired gentleman of military bearing. His clothes were somewhat worn, but his shoes were polished and his suit neatly pressed. He bowed politely to Nancy and introduced himself as Philip March.

"Oh, yes, my father is expecting you. Please come in."

Nancy led the man into the living room where Carson Drew was waiting. When she started to leave, Mr. March invited her to stay and hear his story. He sank wearily into a chair.

"I owe you an apology, Mr. Drew, for asking such a strange favor," he began in a tired voice. "A feeling of desperation came over me this afternoon. On the spur of the moment I decided to come to your office. You and your daughter have helped so many people, I thought you might advise me."

The elderly man was very pale and ill at ease. To give him time to compose himself, Nancy offered to serve coffee. This seemed to refresh him somewhat and Mr. Drew then inquired if the writer of the letters was someone close to him.

"Yes, he was my son. My only son," the caller said sadly. "In fact, he was my only child and a soldier as I once was. But he lost his life four years ago on a routine training mission."

"I'm sorry to hear that," Mr. Drew said sympathetically, and Nancy added a word of condolence.

"Fipp—that's what my Philip called himself

when he was a little boy, and the name stuck," Mr. March went on. "Fipp was married to a lovely girl, but she passed away soon after he did. Then my wife died. Now all I have is little Susan. Her mother entrusted her to my care."

"She is your grandchild?" Nancy asked.

"Yes. Susan is six years old, and I want to keep her with me, but—" The elderly man closed his eyes as if to shut out an unhappy thought. "To bring her up properly I should have a house-keeper. But I can't afford one unless Fipp's music can be found and sold. Besides, I may lose my—our—home. My income is so small."

"Please tell us more about the music," Nancy begged, touched by the man's story.

"Perhaps I should start by briefing you on my family. The Marches have been proud, well-to-do people—several generations of us in River Heights. I'm not going to be the one to ask for charity for my granddaughter. Fipp wouldn't want me to."

As Mr. March paused to take another sip of coffee, Carson Drew inquired how the lost music could bring him any money.

"The songs were never published," the caller replied. "And they were very fine." He turned to Nancy. "The kind of up-to-date music you young people like, but much better than a lot of it I hear."

Nancy was interested at once.

"My son could not bring himself to take the songs to a publisher, for he was never quite satisfied with his work," Mr. March explained. "Then, just before he entered the service, Fipp put the music away in some secret place. If it can only be found and sold, little Susan will be amply provided for."

"Mr. March, what made you think there is a clue to the songs in these letters?" Nancy asked.

"Connie, Susan's mother, wrote to Fipp, suggesting that he tell us where the music was. My boy was full of fun, and replied that he'd give her a hint and she could look for it. Then, after a few more letters"—at this point Mr. March bowed his head—"no others came."

Several moments of silence followed. Finally Mr. Drew spoke. "My daughter and I could not find a clue, but perhaps we can if we study the letters more thoroughly."

"Thank you, thank you," Mr. March murmured. "I'll remember your kindness always. I'd never ask your help for myself—only for Susan. A friend has been caring for her lately, but she's moving away and is bringing Susan back to me the first of the week. I must do something very soon. Susan has no other relatives to take care of her. If I am not financially able to do it, I will have to ask for charity. This would have broken her parents' hearts."

Nancy and her father accompanied their caller to the door, promising to do what they could. As he stepped outside, a rock came whizzing through the air toward him. It struck Mr. March on the head and he slumped to the flagstone walk.

"Oh!" Nancy cried. She rushed outside and bent over the inert form.

Mr. Drew glanced in the direction from which the missile had been hurled. He spotted a man darting from a cluster of bushes that lined one side of the semicircular driveway. At this distance the lawyer knew he could not overtake the fugitive.

Together Nancy and her father carried the stricken figure inside and laid him on the living-room couch. By this time Hannah Gruen, the Drews' motherly housekeeper who had helped rear Nancy, hurried in.

"I think," she said worriedly, "that we should call Dr. Ivers." The others agreed and she went to phone him and also the police to give a full report.

By the time the physician arrived, Mr. March had regained consciousness. After an examination, he said the man need not go to the hospital.

"However, he should not try to travel alone, or drive a car." Dr. Ivers turned to the others. "Mr. March is suffering more from malnutrition than from the lump on his head. What he needs is rest and good food for a few days."

"I have no car," the visitor said. "Can't afford it."

At once Nancy whispered to her father, "Why don't we keep him here?"

The lawyer nodded and conveyed the invitation to Mr. March. At first he hesitated, then accepted weakly. Mr. Drew and the doctor carried him upstairs to the guest room.

"I'll fix a bowl of broth," said Mrs. Gruen, heading for the kitchen. "Make some toast, Nancy," she directed.

When the food tray, which included a broiled hamburger and rice pudding was ready, Nancy carried it upstairs. Mr. March seemed to enjoy the food, then fell asleep, mumbling that he would leave in the morning. But when morning came, Nancy persuaded him to stay by telling him she needed more information about the missing music.

"You rest now, and later we'll go over the letters together," she told him.

During the day Nancy brought up trays of food to Mr. March and encouraged him to talk about himself. She found him to be a delightful, cultured person. The past few years he had not been strong and therefore had been unable to work very much.

"I want you to see my house sometime," he said late that afternoon. "Of course it doesn't look like it used to—I don't make a very good housekeeper, and I haven't been able to afford one, or a gardener either, for a long time."

"How old is the house?" Nancy asked.

"Over two hundred years; at least, part of it is."

"How intriguing!" she exclaimed. "When you're well enough to go home, I'll drive you there and then you can show the place to me."

In the midst of this conversation the doorbell rang. Nancy excused herself, turned on the bedside radio, then hurried downstairs.

"Hi, George and Bess!" said Nancy as she opened the front door wide. She grinned at George. "My goodness, you've had more hair cut off!"

George Fayne was an attractive slender brunette. She tossed her head. "Anyway, Burt Eddleton had better like it."

"Nancy," said her companion, "we came to find out if you plan to get a new dress for the Emerson dance." Bess Marvin, George's pretty, slightly plump cousin, was going to it with Dave Evans.

"I haven't given it much thought," Nancy replied. "I've started helping Dad on a new case, and—"

"And when you're working on a mystery you

have a one-track mind!" George finished with a grin.

"Can you tell us anything about the case?" Bess asked.

Nancy briefed George and Bess about Fipp March's music. The girls were interested and offered their assistance if Nancy should need it.

"I'll keep in touch," Nancy promised.

"And don't forget the dance!" George teased as the cousins said good-by.

Nancy went back to Mr. March's room. Beautiful music was coming from the radio. It was a trumpet solo of a haunting tune with orchestral accompaniment.

Suddenly Mr. March cried out excitedly, "That melody! It was my son's. He never had it published! The song has been stolen! You must find the thief!"

CHAPTER II

Spooky Mansion

"STOLEN?" Nancy repeated. "The music was stolen?"

"Yes, yes," Mr. March vowed, sitting up in bed with a jerk. "The words, the tune, everything!"

The elderly man suddenly clapped his hands to his head. Nancy, fearful he was about to black out, rushed to the bed and eased him back onto the pillows.

"Please don't excite yourself about this," she begged. "Actually it may turn out that it was a good thing you heard this. Let's hope the announcer at least mentions the name of the soloist."

Unfortunately the piece ended without the announcer giving the title of the song or any credits to composer or soloist. For the rest of the day the radio was turned on continuously, in the hope that the song would be played again.

Nancy and Mr. March waited attentively all day, but up to the time he was ready to go to sleep that evening, neither of them heard the melody again. He was positive, though, that it was one of his son's compositions.

"Fipp was very talented," he declared proudly, as Nancy smoothed the bedsheets and turned his pillows. "Why, my son could play six different instruments. When he lived at home, he would lock himself in the attic and compose for hours at a time. Then when the pieces were finished, he would come downstairs to the music room and play them for the family."

"Do you know of anyone who might have stolen your son's work?" Nancy asked thoughtfully. Mr. March shook his head.

The young detective realized that she would have to proceed cautiously in any investigation. She could not accuse a person of plagiarism until there was proof. Her task was now twofold: to locate the thief and trace the rest of the unpublished music. She and Mr. March read Fipp's letters again, but as before, Nancy could find no clue in any of them.

She said slowly, "I suppose you've searched the music room and the rest of your home for your son's songs?"

"Oh, many times. But to no avail."

"How about the attic?"

"I've looked there, too," the man replied. "The songs are missing, and it's my belief now, after hearing the one over the radio, that maybe all of them have been stolen."

Nancy wondered if the person who had tried to harm Mr. March was involved in the theft.

"The man probably followed him. When the assailant learned he was coming to consult a lawyer, he tried to keep him from doing anything more," the young detective said to herself.

No report had been received from the police, so Nancy assumed they had no leads to the attacker.

The next afternoon when the doctor pronounced Mr. March strong enough to go home, Nancy said she would take him there in her car. After an early supper, she invited Bess and George to accompany them.

"I'm sorry to have you see my estate so rundown," the elderly man said as they rode along. "There was a time when it was one of the showplaces of River Heights."

The evening was gloomy. As the car approached the river, dark storm clouds scudded across the sky.

"There's the house—beyond this pine grove. Turn here," Mr. March directed. He was in the front seat of the convertible. "It's called Pleasant Hedges."

The name hardly suited the estate, for the

hedges were untrimmed and entangled with weeds and small stray bushes. Long grass and weeds covered the lawn. Several tall pine trees stood near the house. The wind whispered dismally through the swaying boughs.

"It's spooky," Bess said in a hushed voice to George, who was next to her in the rear seat. "That man who threw the rock at Mr. March may be hiding here waiting to attack us!"

"We'd better keep our eyes open," George answered.

The house was a rambling structure, partly covered with vines. There was a gray stone section at one end, but the rest was built of clapboards, which were badly weather-beaten.

"Now that we're here, may we look inside the house, Mr. March?" Nancy asked as she pulled up at the front door. "Maybe the four of us together can find that lost music."

"I'll be grateful if you'll try," he replied. "Your young eyes no doubt are sharper than mine."

As Nancy gazed at the stone wing, she thought that it appeared to be much older than the rest of the house and asked Mr. March about it.

"That part was built way back when people around here had plenty of servants," he explained. "We'll go in there first."

He led his callers along a weed-grown path to some moss-covered steps.

"The lower level of the old building was a stable," Mr. March explained.

The girls descended the steps, snapped on a light, and looked inside the stable. It was dirty and cobwebby from years of disuse. The long rows of empty stalls, each with a name posted above it, fascinated them.

"Running Mate," Bess read aloud. "And here's another—Kentucky Blue. How interesting!"

"Those were the names of two of my grandfather's horses," Mr. March explained. "Great racers they were in their day. The Marches kept a stable which was known throughout the country. The trainers lived upstairs."

He pointed to a narrow stairway. The girls climbed up, clicked on overhead lights, and glanced into the small bedrooms which ran off a center hallway.

Nancy looked around carefully for any possible hiding places in the walls or floors where Fipp March might have put the music he had composed. She did not see one anywhere.

The three girls descended the antique stairway, which groaned beneath their weight. Mr. March escorted them back to the main entrance of the house. He took a large brass key from his pocket and after several attempts succeeded in unlocking the heavy old door. It swung open with a grating sound.

"The place is pretty bare," the owner said with a sigh. "I've sold nearly all the good furniture. Had to do it to raise money for little Susan."

The girls walked into the long, empty hall, which sent out hollow echoes when the visitors spoke. From there Mr. March led them to the music room. The only furniture in it was an old-fashioned piano with yellowed keys and a thread-bare chair in front of it.

Several other rooms on the first floor were empty and dismal. Heavy silken draperies, once beautiful, but now faded and worn, hung at some of the windows. The dining room still had its walnut table, chairs, and buffet, but a built-in corner cupboard was bare.

"I sold the fine old glass and china that used to be in there," Mr. March said to Nancy in a strained voice. "It seemed best. Come. We'll go upstairs now."

Some of the bedrooms on the second floor were furnished, but they did not contain the lovely old mahogany or walnut bedsteads and bureaus one might have expected. A few inexpensive modern pieces had taken the place of those which had been sold.

Realizing how desperately Mr. March needed money, Nancy kept her eyes open for any objects which could be sold to antique dealers. Apparently almost everything of value had been removed. She asked if the girls might begin their search for the missing music.

"Go right ahead," Mr. March told her.

For the next two hours she, Bess, and George tapped walls, looked into cupboards beside the fireplaces, and examined the flooring for removable boards. Three times Nancy inspected the paneled music room. There seemed to be no clue anywhere.

"Nothing left to check but the attic," said the young detective to Mr. March at last. "May we go up there?"

"I'll show you the way. It's a long, steep climb," he declared, opening the door to a stairway. "I don't go up there very often. It winds me."

After getting a candle, the elderly man conducted the girls to the attic steps.

"There are no lights, but maybe you can see well enough by candlelight."

Nancy chided herself for leaving her flashlight in the car and said she would get it. Just then they heard loud pounding somewhere downstairs.

"What was that?" Bess asked, startled.

"It sounded to me as if someone might be hammering on a door!" George suggested.

Nancy offered to find out, but Mr. March would not hear of this.

"No, I'll go," he insisted. "You girls search the attic in the meantime. I'll leave the candle."

It was so dark in the attic that at first the girls could see little by candlelight. As soon as Nancy's eyes became accustomed to the dimness, she groped her way forward in the cluttered room.

"The attic is really very interesting," she said, surveying the assortment of boxes and trunks. She called her friends' attention to a fine old table which stood in one corner. "I believe Mr. March could sell that," she said. "And look at these old-fashioned hatboxes!"

She picked up one of the round, cardboard boxes. On it was the picture of a gay rural scene of early American life.

"Let me see that!" exclaimed Bess, blowing off the dust. "Mr. March certainly could get something for this. Only yesterday Mother told me about a hatbox like this which brought a good price at an auction sale."

"There are at least a dozen here!" George declared excitedly. "All in good condition, too!"

They were decorated with pictures of eagles and flowers, as well as scenes of American history. Two of them contained velvet bonnets with feather ornaments.

"Girls, this attic may be a valuable find!" Nancy exclaimed.

"Even if we don't locate the missing music, there may be other things here Mr. March can sell," George added. "Let's—"

She stopped speaking as a cry came from below. It was followed by a shout.

Rushing to the stairway, Nancy listened anxiously. She heard Mr. March calling her name in a distressed voice.

"Come quick! I need your help!"

CHAPTER III

Bad News

THOROUGHLY alarmed, Nancy and her friends at once abandoned their search of the attic and hurried down the steep stairway as fast as they could.

"What can be wrong?" Bess gasped.

"Maybe Mr. March has fallen and hurt himself," Nancy suggested.

George's face showed her concern. "Oh, we must find him!"

The girls could not locate the man anywhere on the second floor. Descending to the first, they were relieved to find him uninjured. He was talking excitedly to a middle-aged woman.

"This is Mrs. French, the friend who's been looking after Susan," he explained quickly. He introduced the girls. "She says my little granddaughter is seriously ill."

He pointed to a pathetic-looking child who sat

huddled in a large living-room chair. Her face was red with fever and her dark hair touseled.

"It's not my fault," Mrs. French spoke up. "I've been caring for Susan as I would my own daughter. But all of a sudden she seems to have come down with something."

"I'm sure you're not to blame for Susan's illness," Nancy said kindly as she went toward the little girl. "Let's take Susan to her room and then phone for a doctor."

"I don't feel good," Susan confessed as Nancy carried her up the stairs, followed by Bess and George.

"You'll soon be in your own bed. Then you'll feel better," Nancy said comfortingly.

"Poor little thing," Bess murmured.

"My eyes hurt," the child added wistfully, "and I'm awful hot."

This gave Nancy an idea. When they reached the child's bedroom, she turned the lamp full on Susan.

"Measles," she announced, noting the red blotches. "How well I remember when I had them! Same symptoms."

"Poor Mr. March!" George whispered. "What'll he do?"

"He hasn't enough money to get his granddaughter a nurse," Nancy thought. "And Mrs. French is moving soon and can't take her back."

Aloud she said, "Girls, do you remember Effie?"

"That dizzy maid who works for your family once in a while?" George laughed. "How could one forget her?"

Nancy smiled. "She can be very efficient, as long as she isn't involved in a mystery. I believe I'll see if she can come here."

"This old homestead already has the makings of a mystery," George said significantly.

"Effie would be the solution to the housekeeping problem," Nancy went on. "I hope Mr. March will agree to having her here."

Leaving Bess and George with Susan, Nancy went downstairs to report to Mr. March.

"I'm glad it's nothing worse than that!" he said when Nancy explained to him what the trouble probably was. Mrs. French was also greatly reassured.

"I'll call Dr. Ivers," Nancy offered, "but Susan will soon be asleep, I'm sure. Bess, George, and I will take care of her for the night."

Mrs. French, although eager to be helpful, seemed relieved to be able to pass on the responsibility for Susan's care. After Nancy had phoned the doctor and received instructions, she notified her father that the girls were staying. He offered to inform the Faynes and Marvins.

As soon as Mrs. French left, Mr. March and

Nancy went upstairs to see Susan. The child was resting quietly.

"Measles are not usually serious," Nancy remarked as they returned to the living room. "But Susan will have to stay in bed for a while."

"What am I to do?" the elderly man asked helplessly. "I've never taken care of a sick child. Susan has always been so lively and healthy. I just don't know—" Mr. March broke off in despair.

This was Nancy's opportunity to mention Effie as a possible housekeeper. The problem of salary worried Mr. March.

"I have a surprise for you." Nancy smiled. "Just before you called us from the attic, we found several fine old hatboxes and a table which can be sold. The money from them will take care of things for a while."

Mr. March looked at Nancy gratefully. "You've been so good," he said. "I guess fate led me to your door to ask your help for little Susan."

"As soon as things get straightened out here, I'll go on searching for the music," Nancy promised.

The girls tried to make Susan comfortable with meager supplies in the house. Nancy sat up most of the night, acting as nurse to the feverish child. After breakfast the next morning Bess and George took over. Nancy drove to Effie's house.

The maid, kind-hearted and loyal to the Drew family, was easily persuaded to take charge at

Pleasant Hedges. She packed and left with Nancy. But when Effie glimpsed the huge, barren old dwelling, she almost changed her mind.

"Oh! Oh!" she wailed. "What am I getting into? Another mystery? This old place looks haunted! I believe I'd better go home!"

Nancy finally convinced the girl to stay. As Effie began to work, her fears seemed to vanish. She and Nancy had stopped to buy food, and soon Effie was starting preparations for a hot lunch.

"I've done all I can for the time being," Nancy said wearily to Mr. March, declining his invitation to stay. "Dr. Ivers will be coming soon. The girls and I are going home to get some sleep."

"You more than deserve it," he replied. "I never can thank all of you properly for what you've done."

The girls put the table and hatboxes in Nancy's car and rode away. Nancy dropped Bess and George off at their homes. Then she went on to the Drew house.

"You must be thoroughly exhausted," Hannah Gruen declared.

"I may spend most of the day in bed," Nancy replied. "Later on I'll go down to Mr. Faber's Antique Shop and try to sell Mr. March's things."

When Nancy had completed her errand late that afternoon, she came home with a sizable check for the old table and hatboxes. Mr. Drew praised her, then listened attentively to his daughter's report on the situation at the March mansion.

"Dad, did you hear anything from the police?" Nancy asked.

He shook his head. "I guess that without clues we'll have to forget the stone thrower."

Nancy was up early the following morning. She had just finished a hearty breakfast when Hannah Gruen told her that Effie was on the telephone.

"Effie!" Nancy exclaimed. "I hope nothing is wrong."

She dashed out to the hall to answer the call. At first Effie talked so fast and in such an excited voice that Nancy was unable to determine what was wrong.

"Effie, calm down! I don't understand a word you're saying! Has something happened to Susan?"

"Susan is all right," the maid admitted in a quieter tone.

"Then what is wrong?"

"Everything! Oh, I'm scared! I don't want to stay!"

"Tell me what happened."

"Last night—" Effie paused.

"Yes?" Nancy prompted her.

"I'd better not tell you any more. Please get out here as fast as you can!"

Nancy lost no time in driving to the old March homestead. Effie met her at the door.

"Let's talk outside," the maid whispered. "I don't want Mr. March to hear me. He gets so excited if anything goes wrong."

Nancy suppressed a smile. Effie herself often reacted the same way. She followed the maid to a corner of the lawn.

Effie glanced carefully about her. Then in a half-whisper she began her story.

"It happened late last night. I kept hearing creaking sounds and couldn't sleep. So I got up. I was standing looking out the bedroom window when all of a sudden I saw a big, powerfully built man sneaking across the lawn!"

"Had he come from the house?"

"He must have. He came around from the back and stole off toward the garage. Then he disappeared. Oh, I don't like this place! Can't we take little Susan and go into town?"

"We shouldn't move her while she's ill," Nancy replied. "After all, you don't know that the man was actually in the house. There isn't anything valuable here for anyone to steal."

"I guess that's right," Effie conceded. "And I saw to it that all the doors and windows were locked before I went to bed."

"Suppose we go around now and see if any of

them were forced open last night. Which ones did you open this morning?"

"Only the dining room and kitchen."

Together Nancy and Effie inspected the first floor of the house. Mr. March was upstairs with Susan and unaware of their investigation. After each window had been checked and found to have been untouched by any intruder, Effie was greatly relieved.

"I guess that man wasn't in here after all," Effie said with a sigh.

The maid returned to her work, apparently no longer disturbed. Nancy was far from being satisfied. She went outside to examine the yard. To her dismay she discovered fresh footprints in the soft earth. They circled the house, then led away from a point near the former servants' quarters.

"Effie *did* see someone!" she thought. "But what would a prowler be interested in here?"

Again Nancy followed the circle of footprints around the mansion. Then an alarming thought struck her. "Maybe he has a skeleton key!"

Another idea leaped into Nancy's mind. Perhaps the trespasser had been looking for Fipp March's unpublished music! He might be the one who had stolen the piece Mr. March had heard on the radio!

CHAPTER IV

A Startling Figure

"I'LL renew my search for the missing compositions at once," Nancy decided.

On her way to the attic she stopped to say good morning to Susan and Mr. March. The little girl was sitting up in bed, a big grin on her face. She was listening to her grandfather tell stories.

"The doctor says I'm almost better, Nancy," the child said happily. "I'm sure I can get up soon, and I'm never going away from here again —ever!"

Mr. March's eyes glistened with tears, and Nancy was sure she knew what he was thinking. She opened her purse and took out a check made out to the order of Philip March.

"For me? From Mr. Faber's Antique Shop?" the elderly man asked, not understanding.

"For your table and hatboxes. The ones my friends and I found in your attic."

"I had no idea they were worth so much! This will tide us over for some time."

"And now I'm going to search for something even more valuable—the music." Nancy smiled.

"I'm sure you won't find it," Mr. March declared sadly. "It's been stolen, I'm afraid."

Nancy did not tell him how near the truth she thought he might be. She said nothing about the mysterious prowler. Instead, she urged Mr. March to be hopeful.

Nancy realized the mystery would be a long way toward being solved if the elderly gentleman could identify some of the tunes on radio programs. He had no television set and his one radio did not work very well.

"Mr. March, suppose I bring my portable radio out here tomorrow," she said. "Carry it around with you all the time. You may hear more of your son's songs."

"That's very thoughtful of you."

Nancy straightened the covers on Susan's bed, then said she would start her hunt on the third floor.

"My friends and I didn't have a chance to do much searching in the attic the other day," she told Mr. March. "I guess if the music is in this house, it will be up there."

"You may be right. But be careful."

When Nancy reached the top of the narrow stairway she turned on her flashlight and looked about, wondering where to begin her hunt. The placed seemed even more spooky than the previous time she had been there. There was a musty odor in the attic. As she stepped forward to open a window, the floorboards groaned.

Nancy decided to begin her search in an old horsehide trunk. She lifted the lid and saw a yellowed wedding gown of rich, brocaded satin.

"This lovely dress must have belonged to Susan's grandmother," she thought.

Alongside the gown lay half a dozen old-fashioned pictures. One of them instantly struck Nancy as familiar.

"I believe this is a Currier and Ives! Yes, here's the name to prove it!"

Her heart leaped, for she knew how eager collectors were to buy these old prints.

"What luck this is!" She smiled. "Wonder what else I can find here that could be sold."

Nancy had been so busy she had failed to notice a lowering thunderstorm which had been coming nearer and nearer. Now it broke over the old house in all its fury.

"Guess I'd better close this window and then help shut the ones downstairs," she thought, stepping across several boxes to reach the dormer.

After securing it firmly, she went toward the stairs and started down. Just then she heard a splintering sound, followed by a crash which shook the old March mansion convulsively.

Below was pandemonium. Susan was crying loudly, Effie was shrieking, and Mr. March was shouting:

"Nancy! Nancy, are you all right?"

The girl hurried down and assured him she was unharmed. She in turn was relieved to find the others safe, but Susan was trembling with fright. The little girl had gotten out of bed and scampered into the hall. Now she clung piteously to Nancy.

"I don't want to stay alone!" she wailed. "Something fell on the house by my window."

Nancy stroked the child's head soothingly. She asked what had happened. Mr. March, already on his way down the broad staircase to the first floor, replied that he thought one of the big pine trees had blown over and struck the house.

"The—the lightning did it!" declared Effie, terror in her voice.

"Chin up, Effie," said Nancy. "Let's all of us go downstairs and see what happened."

She got Susan's bathrobe and slippers, then together they followed Mr. March. He called to them to come into the music room. Out of a window they could see one of the tall pines leaning against the mansion. As soon as the rain stopped, Nancy and the elderly man went outside to see what damage the fallen tree had caused.

"Very little harm done," said Mr. March. "This house is well-built. That's a heavy tree. I'm glad it didn't fall on your car, Nancy."

"I am, too," she replied. "If you'd like me to, I'll go to a garage and get some men to bring a wrecker up here and pull the tree away from the house."

"That would be a good idea, but the expense—"

"I know a man who won't charge much," said Nancy. "And that reminds me, I found some more things up in the attic to sell—a dozen or so pictures."

She hurried to the attic and gathered up the old prints.

"Do you recall these?" Nancy asked Mr. March. "They were stored in the horsehide trunk. They'll bring a good price."

"You mean they're worth money?"

"Indeed they are. Mr. Faber will be glad to get them. I've only begun my search of the attic. Let's hope there are many more salable treasures up there."

"I take it you didn't find any of Fipp's music?"

"Not yet. I'll have another look tomorrow," Nancy promised.

As she was about to leave the house, Effie came running toward her.

"Oh, Miss Nancy, you're not going to be away long, are you?" she cried out. "I won't draw a comfortable breath till you return!"

"I'll be back in the morning."

"Morning!" Effie shrieked. "I can't stand it here without you. Creaking sounds, men prowling about at night— Oh, Miss Nancy, please come back and sleep here."

"I'm afraid if it's as bad as you say, I won't be able to sleep." The young detective grinned. "Well, I'll try to get back," she said and went to her car.

Her first stop was Leonard's Garage. The owner had equipment for removing fallen trees and promised to go out to Pleasant Hedges at once. Then Nancy went on to Faber's Antique Shop and received a sizable check for Mr. March. Finally she dropped into her father's office to tell him her plans and also to report what had happened at the March mansion.

"You say Effie saw a man prowling about?" Mr. Drew asked.

"Yes," Nancy replied. "And I found footprints going around the house."

"I don't like that," said Mr. Drew. "If you go back to the mansion, Nancy, I don't want you to take any unnecessary chances."

"I won't."

Nancy hugged her father and left his office. Before going home she bought a few toys for Susan. Later she packed them, together with some groceries, the portable radio and her clothes, in a suitcase. After an early supper she drove back to Pleasant Hedges.

"Oh, I'm so relieved to see you!" Effie cried.

Presently Nancy turned on her radio to a station which was broadcasting popular music. She asked Mr. March to listen carefully.

"Perhaps you'll hear the song you recognized the other night," she suggested. "If you should, please jot down the station, the orchestra, and if it is announced, the name of the composer."

"Nothing would please me more than to expose the impostor!" Mr. March declared. "I want the world to know Fipp wrote that song!"

The elderly man carried the radio upstairs. Meanwhile Nancy decided to do some more hunting in the attic. Unfortunately her flashlight battery was dead, so she went to the kitchen for a candle.

Effie began to chatter. "This house ain't so bad in the daytime, but when it starts gettin' dark, the shadows just sort of leer at you!"

Nancy laughed. "Nonsense!"

She opened a cupboard and took out a long white candle.

Effie looked at her questioningly. "What are you planning to do now?"

"There's no light in the attic," explained Nancy, "and my flashlight battery is dead."

"You're not going up there tonight!" Effie exclaimed, aghast.

"I'm sure nothing will happen to me, Effie, and I want to help Mr. March if I can."

The maid shrugged her shoulders in resignation as Nancy set the candle in a holder. She left the kitchen, went to the second floor, and stopped at the foot of the attic stairway. There she touched a match to the wick and held the candle high in her hand as she ascended cautiously. Just as she reached the top of the steps, the light went out.

Nancy's heart began to pound. Was someone up there? She shook off her momentary fear.

"It was only a draft from that leaky window," Nancy told herself. She struck an extra match and relighted the wick.

Nancy stepped into the attic. The candle flickered again and nearly went out. Something moved.

"My own shadow, of course," she reasoned. "But how grotesque I look!"

Nancy's eyes focused on a massive wardrobe which stood against the far wall.

"I'll search that first," she decided, crossing the attic.

Setting the candle on the floor, she grasped the knob of the door and pulled.

"Wonder what I'll find?" she asked herself.

The door did not give. At the same moment there was a creaking sound. Nancy could not tell where it had come from. She picked up the candle and looked around.

"It's nothing, I'm sure," Nancy told herself, but she could not shake off the uneasy feeling that had come over her.

Once more she put down the candle and tugged at the door. It gave suddenly, swinging outward on a squeaky hinge.

From within, a long bony arm reached out toward Nancy's throat!

CHAPTER V

A Suspected Thief

IT was impossible for Nancy to stifle a scream as the long bony fingers brushed against her throat. She staggered backward. The candlelight flickered wildly.

"Come away! Come away before that—that thing gets you!" shrieked someone behind her.

The voice was Effie's. The maid, worried about Nancy, had followed her to the attic.

"It's nothing. Nothing but a skeleton," said Nancy, her own voice a trifle unsteady.

"It struck you with its bony hand!" quavered Effie. "Oh, I'm getting out of this house tonight, and I'm never coming back!" she announced, starting down the steps.

"Please don't go downstairs and frighten Susan," Nancy pleaded, her own momentary fear gone. "Surely you see what happened?"

"You were attacked by a skeleton!"

"No, Effie. The thing is hanging inside the wardrobe. One hand seems to be attached to a nail on the door. When I jerked it open, the arm swung out and the fingers brushed me."

Nancy reached into the closet and touched the chalk-colored bones.

"What's a thing like that doing here, anyway?" Effie asked in a voice less shaky than before. "I don't like it!"

Before Nancy could reply, they heard footsteps on the attic stairs. Mr. March called, "Anything wrong up there? I heard someone scream."

"We found a skeleton in the wardrobe," Nancy explained. "It startled us."

Mr. March slowly climbed to the attic and went toward the open wardrobe.

"Oh *that!*" he said in relief. "I'd forgotten all about it. Fact is, I didn't know Fipp had put it in the closet."

The elderly man then explained that the skeleton originally had been brought there by a young medical student, a cousin of Fipp's.

"You know how boys are," he added with a chuckle. "They used this skeleton on Halloween, and never did take it away."

"You're sure your son put it here?" Nancy asked thoughtfully.

"Who else could have done it?"

Nancy did not reply. Instead she began an investigation of the wardrobe. She figured it was just possible Fipp March had rigged the strange figure to frighten away all but members of his own family.

Perhaps this was his hiding place for the missing music!

Excited, Nancy held up the candle in order to examine every inch of the old piece of furniture. When a hasty glance revealed nothing but dust and cobwebs, she tapped the sides, top, and bottom for sliding panels. None came to light.

Effie, tired of waiting, coaxed Nancy to go downstairs. Mr. March, concerned about Susan during their long absence, said he thought they should all go below. Nancy did not want to give up the search, but out of deference to the elderly man's wishes, she reluctantly followed the others to the second floor.

"I'm going to look at that old wardrobe again soon," she said to herself. "I have a hunch it holds a strange secret."

For two hours she and Mr. March talked and listened to the radio she had brought. Nancy was disappointed that they had not heard the song which he thought was his son's. Finally at ten o'clock the elderly man arose and smiled at his guest.

"I believe I will go to bed now. Thank you very much for everything."

"I wish the mystery were nearer to being solved," Nancy said, rising also.

Nancy went to the room assigned to her, but could not sleep. She kept thinking about the skeleton and the man Effie had seen outside the house. Time and again she roused at unfamiliar sounds on the grounds and in the house. Then the next time she opened her eyes it was morning.

"Nearly eight o'clock!" she said in astonishment, looking at her watch. "I did get some sleep after all. I believe I'll hurry home and have breakfast with Dad before he goes to his office."

Explaining to Mr. March that she would return later, Nancy drove to her own house. There she found her father in his study examining something under a microscope.

"Oh, hello," he greeted her, looking up from his work and kissing her. "I thought maybe you'd come and eat with your old dad. Any adventures last night?"

"None, except that a skeleton and I got a little chummy."

"What!"

She related all that had happened at Pleasant Hedges, adding that she planned to investigate the wardrobe further.

"That attic is a strange place indeed," Mr.

Drew commented. Then he turned to a problem of his own. "I'm glad you came back, Nancy, or I believe I would have driven out to get you."

"Something wrong?"

"Not exactly. But I'm puzzled. See these?"

He pointed toward his desk. On it lay two white silk women's scarves, which appeared to be identical.

"What in the world are you doing with those?" Nancy asked.

"Another case." Her father smiled. Then he added, "Take a look at these two scarves. Does the material appear exactly the same to you?"

Nancy examined them carefully. "I can see no difference."

"Nor can I, even under a microscope," declared her father.

Nancy fingered the material as Mr. Drew paused. He stared into space, as if puzzled about something.

"What's the problem?" Nancy asked.

"The scarves were manufactured by separate concerns," Mr. Drew explained. "My client Mr. Booker—president of the Booker Manufacturing Company—contends that another company has stolen his formula for making the special material used in them, and could ruin his business."

"What's the name of the other company?"

"The Lucius Dight Corporation."

"I know the place!" Nancy exclaimed. "Mr. Dight's daughter Diane was in one of my classes in school. She's a little older than I am. You say her father has stolen something?"

Mr. Drew looked concerned. "Is Diane your friend, Nancy?" he asked.

"No, Dad, I wouldn't call her that. She goes around with an entirely different crowd. Diane's an attractive-looking girl, but she's spoiled and willful."

"It's fortunate she's not a particular friend," Mr. Drew said, much relieved, "because I'd like you to do a little sleuthing for me on this case."

"I'd love to!"

"I thought so. While you and I eat breakfast, I'll tell you what I heard from Mr. Booker yesterday afternoon."

Father and daughter took their places at the breakfast table. Then Mr. Drew began his story.

"My client Mr. Booker suspects that a former workman of his, named Bushy Trott, was in reality a spy from the Dight factory."

"What a curious name—Bushy Trott!"

"His nickname, I assume. I've seen a photograph of the man. A coarse-looking fellow with wild, bushy black hair."

"So Mr. Booker believes that Bushy worked at the plant only to learn the secret process for making the silk material?"

"Yes, his contention is that the man was sent as a spy by Mr. Dight. Until recently the Dight plant manufactured only synthetic materials, not silk."

"How can I help on the case?" Nancy inquired eagerly.

"I was wondering that myself, until you mentioned knowing Diane Dight. Do you suppose that through her you might be able to look around her father's plant? As a rule, visitors are barred. If I, a lawyer, should go, the owner might become suspicious of my motives."

"I'll be glad to try," Nancy offered. "If I get into the factory, what am I supposed to do? Locate Bushy Trott?"

"Mainly that, yes. And if you can observe the process used to make the silk material like the one used in these scarves, we'll have something to work on," Mr. Drew declared.

"It's a stiff assignment," his daughter mused. "But no harder than the case of the missing music."

"Perhaps if you work on my new project for a while, and then go back to the other one, you'll approach it with a fresh perspective," Mr. Drew suggested.

After her father had gone to his office Nancy pondered how she might get in touch with Diane Dight without arousing the girl's suspicions about her sudden show of friendship. While she was studying the problem, George Fayne dropped in.

"Why the furrowed brow?" George asked.

"I was thinking about how I'm going to cultivate a friendship with Diane Dight," Nancy replied.

"Diane Dight! How you could like that girl is a puzzle to me!" George protested.

"Did I say I like her?" Nancy countered, her eyes twinkling.

"I might have known." George grinned. "You think she's involved in some mystery. Don't tell me she stole Fipp March's music!"

"No, not that. I'd just like to get her to take me through her father's factory."

"She'd never bother," George predicted. "Always too busy talking about herself and the latest dress she's having made at Madame Paray's."

"I don't know that dressmaker."

"Mother's having one made there to wear to a wedding. It's funny you should mention Diane, because she was there the other day when Mother was, and raised a real storm. Diane wanted Madame Paray to stop all her other work and finish a dress so that she could take it away with her."

"So she isn't in town," said Nancy, disappointed.

"I don't know how long Diane is going to be away. Why don't you phone her house and find out?"

"It would be better if I could get the information some other way."

"How about the dressmaker?" George suggested. "Mother has a fitting there at eleven this morning. Suppose you and I go with her."

"A grand idea."

The two girls hurried off to join Mrs. Fayne. They caught her just leaving the house. A little later Nancy was introduced to Madame Paray. Nancy complimented the dressmaker on Diane Dight's clothes.

"Her figaire ees slim and easy to fit," said the dressmaker modestly. "But I'm afraid she diet too much—and ze diet, eet keep you happy or else eet make you cross when you do not eat enough."

"Diane is out of town, isn't she?" Nancy asked.

"She return today on ze two-o'clock train. I am afraid zere will be anozzer scene when she come here to get her gown. Eet ees not finish."

Quickly Nancy saw an opportunity to get in touch with Diane. She offered to meet the girl at the station and tell her that the dress was not ready.

"Oh, would you? Zat would be most kind. And please tó tell Miss Diane also her papa wishes to hear from her as soon as she arrive."

George grinned broadly. Nancy had managed to arrange the perfect setup for herself! After Mrs.

Fayne and the two girls left the dressmaker's, George congratulated her friend.

"I'm so happy, I'm inviting you both to lunch." Nancy grinned. "Then I'll tell you, Mrs. Fayne, what a schemer I am!"

The meal was a delightful one, and immediately afterward Nancy hastened home to change her clothes. When she came downstairs half an hour later, Hannah Gruen looked at her in amazement.

"Wherever are you going so dressed up?"

"I'm going for a drive with the best-dressed girl in River Heights—Diane Dight!" Nancy giggled, gave the housekeeper a hug, and hurried away mysteriously. "Please give Dad that message if he should phone," she called from the garage.

Nancy drove immediately to the station. The two-o'clock train was just coming in. Quickly she parked the car and dashed across the platform.

The first passenger to step down was Diane Dight. As Nancy went toward the girl, her heart beat faster.

Was her plan going to work?

CHAPTER VI

Nancy's Ruse

"HELLO, Diane!"

The Dight girl looked up, startled, and barely acknowledged the greeting.

"I have a message for you," Nancy said.

"For me? What is it?" Diane questioned apprehensively.

"Madame Paray asked me to tell you that your dress is not ready."

"Oh!" Diane relaxed. Then her eyes snapped. "That woman makes me tired. I wouldn't go to her any more, except that she does make attractive clothes."

"You always look stunning, Diane," said Nancy.

For the first time Diane seemed to take note of what Nancy was wearing. "I like the dress you have on. Did you have it made?"

"Yes, I did," Nancy replied lightly, stifling a desire to smile. She was thinking how pleased Hannah Gruen would be to hear her handiwork so highly praised. Aloud she said, "I'll be glad to drive you, Diane. Let me help you with your suitcase."

Diane protested, but Nancy merely smiled. She took the bag and went to her car. Diane began complaining about the fact that there were never any porters around and that the family chauffeur was on vacation. When they got into the car, Nancy turned in the direction opposite the one to the Dight residence.

"You're going the wrong way!" Diane cried indignantly.

Nancy quickly interjected, "I just recalled that your father wants to see you at his factory right away. Madame Paray asked me to give you that message also."

Nancy kept going until she reached a cluster of brick buildings. There Diane said good-by, adding that she would take a taxi home. But Nancy was not to be put off so easily.

"Oh, I don't mind waiting," she insisted. "I have nothing else to do at the moment."

Before Diane had a chance to object, Nancy was out of the car and walking into the building with her. Out of politeness Diane was forced to introduce her to Mr. Dight's secretary.

"I don't know how long I'll be with my father," Diane told Nancy. She added curtly, "Please don't bother to wait."

After she had disappeared into the inner office, Nancy smiled at Miss Jones, the secretary.

"This must be a fascinating place to work," she said. "Do you know all about the process of making synthetic material?"

"I know a good deal, but far from everything," the young woman replied pleasantly.

"I'd love to go through the plant sometime. Do you suppose Diane would take me?" Nancy inquired.

Miss Jones smiled. "She doesn't seem to be interested in her father's business. If you would like to take a quick look, I'll show you what I can. Of course many of the processes used here are kept secret. Some I don't even know myself."

Nancy's pulse leaped. She could hardly wait to start her trip through the factory, but she tried to appear calm.

"That's sweet of you, Miss Jones," she said. "If you really can spare the time, I'd love to look around."

"As a rule, visitors are not permitted, but since you're a friend of Miss Dight"—here she appraised Nancy's dress with a complimentary look —"I'll be glad to take you through."

As she and Miss Jones walked along the halls

and up and down flights of stairs, the secretary explained the rudiments of the making of synthetic cloth.

"It seems like magic," she said "that coal and oil can be turned into lovely soft materials so quickly. At other factories oil and coal are made into colorless chemicals which we buy. Then they are put into tanks like the one you see over there and churned with chemical compounds for several hours."

"Is the result raw fiber solutions?" Nancy asked.

"Yes. Each is given a different trade name depending on mixture and composition."

"Nothing secret about that," thought Nancy.

As Miss Jones led her farther into the plant, Nancy kept her eyes open for Bushy Trott. Although there were many workmen busy at their tasks, she saw no one who resembled the suspected thief.

One thing she did take note of was a heavy door on the stairway landing at the far end of the building. A metal sign on it read:

POSITIVELY NO ADMITTANCE.
DANGER. KEEP OUT.

"I wonder if that is one of the secret places Miss Jones spoke about," Nancy speculated to herself. "Maybe Bushy Trott is in there!"

Soon they reached the top of another stairway,

and the secretary outlined the next process in making synthetics.

"Ahead of you is the machine known as the spinneret," she said. "That's what makes thread."

"It's remarkable!" Nancy exclaimed, pretending to be watching nothing but this.

At that moment a bell rang several times.

"That's for me," said Miss Jones. "I guess Mr. Dight wants me. We'll have to go back."

"If you don't mind, I'd like to look around a little longer," Nancy said.

"Well, I don't know." The woman paused. "You really shouldn't. But stay if you wish. If I see Miss Dight, I'll tell her you're here."

Nancy nodded and thanked Miss Jones for the tour. As soon as the secretary left the spinneret room, Nancy moved quickly up the stairway toward the forbidden room.

"I wish I could look in there," she thought.

As Nancy hesitated outside, the door suddenly opened. A workman in soiled dungarees came out, carrying a package which looked as if it might contain a bolt of cloth.

Although the door remained open only an instant, Nancy obtained a fleeting glimpse of the interior. She saw several large chemical vats. Beside one of them, his back to her, stood a man with bushy black hair.

"Bushy Trott!" Nancy thought excitedly. "The man who used to work at the Booker factory!"

The door slammed shut, and she saw no more. Nancy deliberately loitered until the workman who had come out of the room disappeared down the hall.

"I must get a better look at that fellow with the bushy hair!" she decided. "This is my chance to help Dad solve the mystery!"

Glancing quickly around and seeing no one, Nancy cautiously tried to open the door. To her dismay it had a snap lock and would not budge.

"I must get in there!" Nancy thought with determination. In a moment she smiled to herself. "I think I know how to do it!"

Pressing her lips close to the crack of the door to the secret room, Nancy screamed. The ruse was successful. From within came hurrying footsteps.

The next instant the door swung open. Nancy staggered inside, her hand over her half-closed eyes.

"Water," she murmured. "Water."

The big, bushy-haired man who had opened the door stared at her doubtfully.

"Are you sick?" he asked in a coarse, heavy voice.

Nancy did not want to answer questions. To avoid them she pretended to faint. The act was well-timed, for the man, frightened, immediately rushed into the hall for help. The young detective smiled.

"I'll bet that's Bushy Trott! When I describe him to Dad, he'll know for sure."

No sooner had the door swung shut behind the man than she leaped to her feet. Eagerly she gazed about. The room resembled a laboratory. Near her were several vats of rainbow-hued solutions.

Nancy had no opportunity to look further. Heavy footsteps warned her that the man was returning. She barely had time to stretch out on the floor before he came into the room.

As the big, burly figure bent over her, Nancy pretended to revive. Opening her eyes, she gazed up into his ugly, cruel face.

"Here, drink this!" he commanded.

Nancy took a sip of water from the paper cup he offered her.

"I'm feeling better now," she murmured, sitting up.

"You don't work here," he said, scanning her face closely. "How did you get into this part of the factory?" he asked gruffly.

Before Nancy could reply, the outside door swung open again. A stout, well-dressed man with piercing brown eyes stepped inside. Seeing Nancy, he paused in surprise.

"Tro—" He stopped, then went on, "What is

"Water," Nancy murmured. "Water."

the meaning of this? Why have you allowed a visitor here?"

"It's none o' my doin', Mr. Dight," his employee muttered. "She came in herself—said she was feelin' sick."

"Then a little fresh air will help you, miss," Mr. Dight said stiffly.

Taking Nancy firmly by the arm, he assisted the girl to her feet, and escorted her down the stairs into the main section of the factory.

"Who are you?" he asked.

Nancy explained she had brought Diane from the station, but did not give her name.

"It's dangerous for you to wander about this building by yourself. You must never do it again," he remarked in an icy tone of voice.

Nancy thought Lawrence Dight seemed to be frightened. Had she stumbled upon his secret?

When they approached the main entrance, he left her and Nancy headed for the parking lot. Diane was waiting beside Nancy's car.

The two spoke little on the way to Diane's house. After accepting the girl's thanks, Nancy said good-by, then drove at once to her own home.

"Dad!" she greeted her father as she ran into the house. "I had some real luck today! I think I've found Bushy Trott!"

Mr. Drew dropped his newspaper. "Say that again!" he requested.

Nancy repeated her statement and quickly related the entire story of her visit to the Dight plant. Mr. Drew readily identified the suspect from Nancy's description of him. He was deeply impressed with his daughter's work, and smiled when he heard of her ruse.

"Nancy, you're a fast worker and a thorough one!" he complimented her. "If that man actually is Bushy Trott—and you say Mr. Dight started to speak his name—then my case seems to be shaping up."

"What's the next move?"

"I'll arrange to have the man watched. We'll learn everything we can about him."

"Is there something else I can do?" Nancy asked.

"You've already helped me a lot," Mr. Drew replied. "If there's anything more, I'll let you know."

What she had discovered in the factory had increased Nancy's interest in her father's case. She hoped that soon she would be able to follow up more clues for him. In the meantime she must tackle the problems surrounding Mr. March's mystery.

"Watch your step in that old attic," Mr. Drew warned his daughter. "No telling what's there."

"I promise, Dad," she said, smiling.

The following afternoon Nancy returned to the

mansion. Susan and her grandfather were listening to the radio in the little girl's bedroom. As Nancy entered, the orchestra was playing a gay, new melody. As the sweet strains continued, Mr. March cried out:

"That's it! That's one of my son's compositions! I can't remember the name of it, but I certainly recall the tune."

"It's called 'Song of the Wind,' " Nancy said.

"Who do they say wrote it?" he demanded.

"I can't recall," Nancy confessed. When the composer's name was not announced, she said, "Suppose I run downtown and buy a copy of the sheet music?"

Mr. March urged her to hurry, and could hardly wait for her return.

"The composer is Ben Banks," she told him as soon as she got back.

"Ben Banks! Ben Banks!" Mr. March shouted angrily. "Who's he? The man is a thief! That song was Fipp's!"

Nancy promised to try locating Ben Banks. She would get in touch with the publisher of "Song of the Wind," and ask for information about the so-called composer.

"I'll never rest until that rascal is found and exposed!" Mr. March stormed. "Why, the upstart! Not only does he rob the dead, but he cheats Susan out of her rightful inheritance!"

The elderly man's tirade went on and on. To quiet him, Nancy offered to play the selection on the piano, so the two went downstairs to the music room.

The old piano was badly out of tune and she soon gave up. Nancy had just begun to sing the lovely song to Mr. March when from upstairs came a bloodcurdling shriek for help!

CHAPTER VII

Black Widow

NANCY raced upstairs two steps at a time. Susan was in her bed, cowering under the covers.

"Thank goodness she's all right!" Nancy thought and sped on to the attic.

"Who's up there?" she called.

"Me! Effie!"

Nancy doubled her steps. She found the maid alone, jumping about. She was waving her left hand in the air and wailing pitifully.

"I've been bit! I've been bit!" she screamed.

"What bit you?" Nancy demanded.

"The skeleton! Do something, quick!"

"Effie, be sensible. What was it that bit you?"

"It was that skeleton, I tell you!" Dramatically the maid pointed to the bony figure which leaned forward at a rakish angle from the open door of the wardrobe closet. "He just reached out and bit my finger! Oh, the thing is alive!"

Nancy examined Effie's finger, but in the dim light could see no evidence of a wound. She wondered if the girl's imagination had been playing tricks on her.

Nancy heard footsteps on the stairway and called down, "Don't bother to come up, Mr. March. Everything is all right, I guess."

"Except me," Effie wailed.

"Let's go downstairs," Nancy said to the maid. "I'll check your finger again. By the way, what were you looking for in the wardrobe?"

"Some clean linen to change the beds. There's hardly any in the house. Oh, my whole arm hurts now!"

When they reached the second floor, Nancy examined the maid's hand. She received a distinct shock, and Effie herself began to sob loudly.

"Look at it! I'm going to die!" she cried.

This remark brought Susan to the hall. She and her grandfather gazed in awe at Effie's swollen forearm and the tiny puncture in her index finger.

"What did that?" the child asked in fright.

Nancy did not reply to the question. Instead she gently told Susan to get back into bed. Quickly she asked Mr. March for a large handkerchief and tied it tightly about Effie's upper arm.

"We'd better take her to a doctor," she said. "There isn't anything here with which to take care of this wound." To Mr. March she whispered, "I'm afraid a poisonous spider bit Effie."

Nancy drove speedily to the office of Dr. Ivers. Fortunately he was in. He confirmed Nancy's diagnosis, adding that the spider probably was a black widow.

"One rarely finds them in this part of the country," he said, getting a hypodermic needle and filling it with an antidote. By now Effie looked and acted quite ill.

The physician patted her shoulder and tried to keep the girl's mind off herself. He said, "There's another dangerous spider, the tarantula, but that isn't native to these parts either."

Effie began to moan, saying she knew her young life was over.

"Nonsense," said Dr. Ivers. "Fortunately, Miss Drew put the tourniquet on, and you won't suffer as much as you might have otherwise. You'd better keep quiet for a couple of days, though."

"How am I going to do my work?" Effie asked.

"Don't worry about that," Nancy spoke up quickly. "I'll help you."

The doctor gave Nancy instructions for taking care of Effie, and told the patient not to be alarmed. He also advised that the old house be searched thoroughly for the black widow spider.

"I believe I'll go home and get Mrs. Gruen,"

Nancy told Effie as they drove off. "She can come out for a few hours to help us."

The Drews' housekeeper was glad to be of assistance. As soon as they reached the March home, she and Nancy went immediately to the attic, carrying an insecticide spray gun and a broom. There they brushed down dozens of webs and caught every spider they could locate.

"We've found none except the common house variety." Nancy sighed. "Where *could* the black widow have crawled to?"

"I'm not going to let you stay here unless we find it," Hannah Gruen said firmly.

Nancy tried to dispel the woman's fears by saying, "Effie must have scared him off!" But she was worried. Perhaps an intruder had left the deadly spider there as a warning!

The most likely person was the one who had stolen Fipp March's original music! Was he Ben Banks?

"I must write to the publisher of 'Song of the Wind' at once for the address of Ben Banks," Nancy determined. "In all the excitement I completely forgot him."

"Oh!" Hannah Gruen said suddenly.

Crack! Her broom came down with a whack on a spider which had just crawled from beneath the wardrobe. Nancy used the spray gun.

"It's the black widow!" Nancy cried jubilantly. "Now you'll have nothing to worry about."

"Unless there are more of these poisonous creatures up here," declared Mrs. Gruen.

She agreed, however, that it probably would be safe for Nancy to stay, but cautioned her to be extra careful.

While the housekeeper prepared supper, Nancy hurriedly wrote a note to the publisher of "Song of the Wind." Then she went to make Effie comfortable. The maid was feverish and declared her arm itched dreadfully. When she finally dropped off to sleep, Nancy tiptoed away to see that Susan was all right.

The little girl looked up and said, "A bad spider bit Effie. She told me all about it."

Nancy was provoked to learn the maid had told the story to Susan, but she merely smiled. "That's right, Susan, but only good spiders live around here. The bad one is dead now."

To get the child's mind off the unfortunate subject, she told her about the funny antics of the jumping spiders and the flying variety.

"Some of them are just like trapeze performers in a circus," Nancy explained. "They spin a thread and then let the wind carry them through the air. Sometimes they go all the way from shore to a ship at sea."

"Oh, that kind of spider would be lots of fun

to watch!" Susan remarked, her fears gone now.

Hannah Gruen brought up a tray of food for the little girl. Nancy decided that while Susan was eating supper, Mr. March might sit with her, and she would drive Hannah home. When they reached the Drew house, Bess and George were just leaving.

"Where in the world have you been, Nancy?" George remonstrated. "We thought something had happened to you. How about having dinner at my house and telling us about your new mystery?"

Nancy thanked her, but explained why she could not accept the invitation. Bess exclaimed in horror when she heard about the black widow episode.

"You'd better stay out of that place," she advised.

"I'll be careful. Don't worry," Nancy replied. She told the girls to climb into her car and she would drop them off.

Nancy left her friends at George's house and went on. After stopping to buy a flashlight battery, she drove to the March estate and was in time to tuck Susan into bed. The little girl looked up at her wistfully.

"I wish you'd always stay with me," she confided. "You're my best friend."

Nancy leaned down and kissed her. "I'm going

to be here for a while," she promised. "Suppose we pretend each day is a year."

Susan liked this game, and soon she went to sleep happily. Nancy joined Mr. March on the first floor, where he was listening to the radio. As they ate supper together, he told her more about his family.

"I guess my son Fipp came by his musical ability naturally," Mr. March said. "My mother wrote songs for the sheer joy of it. They were composed only for the family though, and never got beyond manuscript form. My son used parts of the melodies in his work. The piece called 'Song of the Wind' was based in part on one that my mother wrote years ago."

Nancy pounced eagerly on this bit of information. It might prove to be good evidence in case of a lawsuit!

"What became of your mother's old songs?" she asked quickly.

"I couldn't say. A few of the pieces may have been put away in the attic. I'm sure Fipp didn't have them. The old melodies had been hummed to him so many times he knew them by heart."

The clue was sufficient to start Nancy on another intensive search. As soon as she washed the dishes, Nancy put the new battery in her flashlight and went to the attic. She began poking around in boxes. One of these was filled with interesting newspapers, some of which dated back a hundred years.

"I'm reading more than I'm working," the young detective scolded herself with a laugh. "I'd better get on with the hunt."

Going hurriedly through the remaining papers, Nancy came at last to the bottom of the box. Her gaze fastened upon a ribbon-tied roll of parchment.

"This may be the very thing I'm after!" she thought excitedly.

Unwrapping it, she discovered the sheet contained the music and words of a song! She hummed the first few bars. They were not familiar.

She started to investigate another box which stood nearby. As Nancy eagerly plunged her hand down, something sharp buried itself in her finger. With a sinking heart Nancy wondered if she might have been poisoned the way Effie had been!

Gingerly she pushed aside the papers, looking for a black widow spider. Then Nancy laughed as she saw what had pricked her finger. Men's antique shoe buckles!

"What gorgeous ones!" she thought, lifting out several pairs of the old silver ornaments. They were studded with semiprecious stones, one of which had a sharp prong on it.

Nancy was happy over the find. The buckles

would bring a nice sum of money for Mr. March. After wrapping them carefully in paper, she put the buckles in her pocket.

At that instant the flashlight which Nancy had laid on the floor rolled away and clicked off. As she leaned forward to pick it up, something landed with a soft thud against her hand.

Out of nowhere floated a few eerie notes of music like the faint strumming of a harp.

CHAPTER VIII

The Strange Secret

NANCY, in the pitch-black attic, kept perfectly still. She hardly breathed. Chills ran up and down her spine.

The music had ceased, but from nearby came the sounds of stealthy footsteps. These were followed by muffled rapping sounds.

"There isn't a harp or a piano here," Nancy told herself, trying to regain her composure. "Maybe this is just a trick to keep people out of the attic."

The rapping had stopped now. Nancy reached again for the flashlight. This time she found it, but to her dismay it would not light.

"The store clerk must have sold me a defective battery," Nancy said to herself, frowning.

She was too far from the stairway to get there safely in the dark among the maze of boxes and trunks.

"What am I going to do?" Nancy thought.

Suddenly she heard her name murmured. "Na-a-ancy! Na-a-ancy!"

"It must be Mr. March," she concluded as the call became louder. "Thank goodness. Now there'll be a light."

She stood up, then froze to the spot as a new thought struck her. If someone really were in the attic, he might harm anyone coming up the steps! Summoning all her courage, Nancy called out loudly:

"I'm in the attic. Don't come up! Just hold a light for me at the foot of the stairs!"

Nancy had expected a hand to be clapped over her mouth, but nothing happened. In relief she called out again, saying her flashlight was not working.

A few seconds later a light shone up the stairway. Mr. March was speaking to her cheerily.

Nancy gingerly found her way across the attic. Soon she was back on the second floor. Mr. March took hold of her arm.

"You're white as a sheet," he said. "Something happened. What was it?"

"Did anyone touch the piano downstairs?" she asked.

"The piano? No. Why?"

"I thought I heard a few notes of music," Nancy replied.

"You're not telling me all you know," the elderly man said. "I want to hear everything. Don't keep anything back."

"I'm afraid somebody or something is in the attic," Nancy admitted. "After my flashlight went out there were all kinds of ghostly noises."

Mr. March grunted. "I'll fix him," he said and started up the stairs. Nancy tried to hold him back.

"I've faced the enemy before," he declared, holding the candle aloft. "And it's high time I find out about that mysterious attic."

Nancy followed him. To her chagrin they found no one, nor was there any evidence of a secret entrance through which an intruder might have come. On the floor near the spot where she had stood lay a large toy bear.

"It must have fallen from the rafters," Nancy decided. She told Mr. March this was one of the strange events that had occurred in the past fifteen minutes. "I guess the bear fell on me," she added.

"That bear belonged to Fipp," his father explained. "I haven't seen it for years."

Nancy was apologetic for having worried him. She picked up her flashlight and said no more about the incidents. But she knew that she had not imagined the stealthy footsteps, the rapping sounds, and the musical notes. Who and what had made them remained a deep mystery.

"Here's a surprise for you," she said, changing the subject. "I located one of the old songs under a pile of newspapers."

Mr. March scanned the parchment eagerly. Finally he spoke. "Oh, yes, I remember this—'The Old and the New.'" He nodded, humming a few bars of the tune. "My mother composed the tune and Fipp later added to it. It was one of his finest."

"It's the best find we've made yet," said Nancy after they had gone downstairs. "If Ben Banks has published a song with this melody, you'll certainly have a case against him."

"I hope you receive a reply to your letter very soon," the elderly man said. He sighed, adding, "This suspense is rather hard on an old fellow like me."

Nancy spoke a few words of encouragement and showed him the valuable old shoe buckles. Then she said good night. That weekend she was kept busy with the housework, and had no chance to go to the attic. But she took time on Saturday to run into the business section of River Heights to see Mr. Faber.

The dealer gave her a good price for the buckles. Mr. March was overjoyed at the encouraging news.

"How wonderful!" he exclaimed. "Oh, Nancy, I'll never be able to repay you for your kindness."

Nancy brushed aside the comment modestly. She knew that the money she had been able to acquire was still not sufficient to take care of Susan or the house expenses indefinitely.

By Monday Effie was able to assume the duties of the household once more, and Nancy returned to her own home. Mr. Drew greeted her cheerily.

"Well, I'm glad to see my daughter again," he said affectionately. "I believe I should take the day off and celebrate."

Knowing she was being teased, Nancy asked, "*Are* you taking a holiday?"

"I'm on my way to see Mr. Booker," her father replied.

Nancy queried him about what progress he had made in clearing up the mystery of the stolen formula for creating the lovely silk material.

"Absolutely none," Mr. Drew confessed. "Men have been shadowing the Dight plant ever since you were there, but they haven't seen Bushy Trott go in or come out of the building."

"Maybe he lives there. Would you like me to go back to the factory and find out?" Nancy asked.

"Not yet, but I may call on you later. Mr. Booker is so sure his process is being imitated that whether or not Trott is there, he wants me to start suit against Lawrence Dight."

"Will you do it?"

"Not until I have a little more evidence," the

lawyer replied. "One has to be mighty careful when accusing a person of Mr. Dight's standing. Up to now Mr. Booker hasn't explained much about how he makes the special silk material, so I'm on my way to find out. Want to go with me?"

"You won't have to ask twice!"

"Then we'll be on our way. Later, if one of us gets into the secret section of the Dight plant, we'll be able to compare the two methods."

Nancy and her father were welcomed cordially by Mr. Booker, who was eager to conduct the Drews through his plant.

"First I'll show you the Gossamer Garment Room," he declared, leading the way.

The Gossamer Room contained several bolts of filmy white silk material like that used in the scarves Nancy had seen. Others were in various colors, while a few were patterned with artistic and unusual designs.

"They're beautiful!" Nancy exclaimed.

Clever designers had fashioned some of the materials into attractive dresses, which hung row upon row in dustproof glass cases.

"I've never seen anything so lovely!" Nancy said. A pale-yellow evening gown caught her eye. "What a stunning dance dress!"

In texture it was unlike anything she had ever seen before. "The material is strong," she said, "yet it looks delicate enough to dissolve at a touch of the hand!"

"That's why we call it gossamer," Mr. Booker said proudly. "I'll show you how it's made. You must promise, of course, never to reveal my secrets!"

"You can trust us!" said Mr. Drew.

The factory owner unlocked a heavy metal door and led his callers into a room where two men sat at tables, engaged in a most unusual occupation.

"This is my spidery," Mr. Booker explained. "Here I breed orb weavers under glass. They provide me with the silk threads I need for my material."

"You actually use spiders!" Nancy gasped.

"Yes." Mr. Booker smiled. "They are very useful to man when one understands how to put them to work."

Nancy watched curiously. One of the men was holding a spider in a pair of forceps. The little insect was exuding a filmy thread from its spinneret. With his other hand the man was winding the silk onto a spool.

"The spiders work fast," Mr. Drew remarked.

"One of them can spin a web half a yard across in less than an hour," Mr. Booker revealed. "Now I'll show you how we make the thread strong enough to be woven into cloth."

Nancy and her father were escorted to the room

where the secret chemical formula was mixed. Not only did Nancy look at the solution in the various tubes, but she took particular note of the peculiar scent it produced.

"I'd be more likely to recognize the odor than anything else. If this chemical is being used at the Dight factory, maybe I can identify it that way," Nancy thought.

Mr. Drew inquired if this was the department where Bushy Trott had worked.

"Yes," Mr. Booker replied, "he was in this section. He came to me highly recommended as a chemist. Because he left my employ abruptly, I suspect that he was sent here as a spy."

Mr. Drew told the manufacturer there was plenty of evidence now against the rival concern.

"We're still trying to check on Bushy Trott," he said. "The next step will be to find out how Lawrence Dight is making his silk material'

"If only I could get into his factory again!" Nancy remarked to her father as they drove away from the Booker plant.

"Couldn't you arrange for another trip with your friend Diane?"

"She's scarcely a friend, Dad. But I'll think up a way," Nancy promised.

After dropping her father at his office, she had an inspiration. If her scheme worked, she would get into the factory!

On impulse she drove directly to the Dight home to put her plan into action. The spacious grounds were located at the edge of the city and were screened from the road by a high, ivy-covered fence. Nancy turned into the winding driveway and coasted to the big white house.

CHAPTER IX

A Blue Bottle

HOPEFULLY Nancy rang the bell at the Dight house. She was eager to carry out her plan. Diane opened the door.

"Have you come to see me?" Diane inquired curtly.

Nancy smiled graciously and replied, "You have a little sister, I believe."

"Jean's seven."

"Then she's only a little bigger than a girl I know who has very few clothes. Do you suppose your mother would be willing to pass on a few of Jean's clothes that she has outgrown?" Nancy asked.

"I'll ask her," Diane offered with a shrug. "Come in."

The invitation delighted Nancy. This was her chance to see what kind of art objects the Dights favored. Perhaps they would be interested in buying some of Mr. March's antiques. If she could obtain something to sell them, she might have a reason for calling on Mr. Dight at his office.

Left alone, Nancy gazed with interest about the luxuriously furnished living room. Against one wall stood a mahogany case with glass shelves. On them was an array of beautiful, unusual old bottles.

"The very thing!" Nancy thought in delight.

She went over to examine the collection. One had the face of George Washington etched in it, another that of Dolly Madison. As Nancy stood gazing at a lovely old blue perfume bottle, Diane came downstairs.

"There you are," she said, tossing a heap of garments onto a sofa. "Mother says to take them all if you like."

Nancy thanked her for the clothing, and then expressed interest in the bottle collection.

"Oh, that's Mother's hobby," Diane replied indifferently. "She spends a great deal of her time at antique stores trying to pick up bargains. She'd rather have an old bottle than something new."

"Many old things are far prettier than new ones," Nancy remarked.

"I don't think so. And especially bottles. Anyway, it's my opinion one collector in the family is enough."

Nancy was tempted to make a retort, but wisely kept still. Diane certainly was a disrespectful and conceited daughter.

"Thank you for the dresses," she said, gathering them up. "Little Susan will be delighted to have them."

From the Dight home Nancy drove directly to Pleasant Hedges. She had seen some old bottles in the attic there!

Nancy showed Mr. March the dresses she had obtained for Susan. They were very pretty, and gave no evidence of having been worn.

"Mrs. Dight was good to send my granddaughter such fine clothes," he said gratefully, "but I can't accept charity."

"That isn't necessary."

"You mean there's some way I can show my appreciation?" he asked.

"In your attic are several nice old bottles. They're standing way back under the eaves," Nancy told him. "Mrs. Dight collects bottles. I'll see that she gets one, if you like, in return for these dresses."

"Do that. I remember the bottles, now that you speak of them."

"May I sell some of them?" Nancy asked.

"Yes, yes. Every penny helps. You might give the blue flowered one to Mrs. Dight."

Excited that her scheme had worked so far,

Nancy went to the attic. Though the sun was pouring in through the one small window, she had to light a candle in order to look in the far corners of the room.

Finally she came to the bottles. There were four which were fairly large in size and several smaller ones. All were exquisite.

Nancy lifted up the bottles one by one. The color of the glass indicated that they were old and valuable.

"This must be the blue one Mr. March spoke about!" she said, examining the bottle. "It's beautiful. Mrs. Dight is lucky to get this in exchange for a few dresses!"

Placing all the glassware in a box, she started for the stairway.

"Oh, I hope my plan works!" She sighed. "I can accomplish two missions if all goes well!"

With Effie's help Nancy washed each bottle until it shone.

"What are you going to do with these?" the maid asked.

"Try to sell them to the husband of a woman who collects old bottles," Nancy said.

She spent most of the afternoon reading and talking to Susan. After she had said good-by to Mr. March and his granddaughter, Nancy went to pick up the old bottles in the kitchen.

"You're coming back tonight?" Effie asked fearfully. "I don't feel well enough to stay here without you, what with ghosts and prowlers hanging around the place."

"We haven't seen a real ghost yet!" Nancy laughed.

"Call it what you like. You can't fool me," the girl complained. "I see a man prowling around, and I'm supposed to believe he was just crossing the lawn on his way home. Then a skeleton happens to be hanging in a closet. Next a black widow crawls out and bites me!"

Nancy, to allay Effie's fears, promised to come back and spend the night.

"I'll get here as soon as I can, Effie," she said.

Taking all the bottles with her, she drove to River Heights. Parking her car at a distance from the Dight factory, Nancy proceeded on foot.

When the young detective reached the plant, it was approaching the closing hour. Workmen were already coming through the gates. Nancy stopped a minute to look for Bushy Trott, but when he did not appear, she headed for the executive offices.

"Am I too late to see Mr. Dight?" Nancy inquired of Miss Jones, the private secretary.

"He's still in his office," the pleasant young woman replied. "I think he'll see you."

The secretary went inside. A moment later she returned to escort Nancy into his private office.

Lawrence Dight arose as Nancy entered, but did not appear too pleased to see her again.

"Mr. Dight, I must apologize for bothering you," Nancy began, deftly whisking the fine blue bottle from the box. "I'm afraid I annoyed you the last time I was here."

The factory owner's gaze fastened upon the beautiful old glass.

"Where did you get that?" he asked, raising his eyebrows in amazement.

"It's a little gift I brought for your wife, Mr. Dight. She very kindly did a favor for me today." Nancy held the bottle so the sunlight pouring through a window shone directly through it. "I have several others here I thought you might like to buy for her collection."

Mr. Dight examined the blue bottle. His cold manner left him for a moment as he admired it.

"Thank you. I'll take it to Mrs. Dight. Let me see the others."

Nancy set them on his desk.

"How much do you want for them?"

Nancy hardly heard him. She was standing near an open window. Glancing down into an alley between the office building and another brick structure, she noticed a familiar figure. The man was Bushy Trott!

"I said, name your price," Lawrence Dight repeated in an irritated voice.

Nancy did not want to lose an opportunity of seeing where Bushy Trott was going. Probably he was heading for the secret section where the stolen formula was being used. This was her chance to find out about it!

"Suppose I leave the bottles with you, Mr. Dight," she said hurriedly, moving toward the door. She tried to act as if she were not eager to get away. "No doubt you would like to examine the glassware before deciding what you would want to pay for it."

To the surprise of Mr. Dight, Nancy opened the door and walked out. In a moment she was at the main exit of the building. Hurrying to the alley, Nancy was just in time to see the suspect enter a small brick building.

No one else was in sight.

"If only I can get in there!" Nancy thought.

Cautiously she tested the door. Although equipped with an automatic lock, it fortunately had not slammed tightly shut. Nancy slipped inside.

The building seemed to be deserted. There were no sounds of workmen or machinery.

Moving noiselessly down a dimly lighted narrow hall, Nancy spied Bushy Trott. He paused for a moment before another door, then quickly opened it and entered.

Nancy did not hesitate. As soon as his footsteps

The suspect entered the building

died away, she followed him through the doorway. The man was not in sight.

Finding herself in a room filled with vats of liquid, Nancy decided to investigate them. But before she had a chance to do so, a key grated in a lock.

Ducking behind one of the vats, she again saw Trott, who entered through another door. He closed and locked it, then went back into the hall again.

Nancy arose and looked into the vats. The color appeared familiar. She sniffed. The odor from the mixture was the same as that which she had smelled at the Booker factory!

"Now I have real evidence!" she exulted.

CHAPTER X

Dangerous Adventure

DELIGHTED with her discovery, Nancy now was intent on finding a container to get a sample from the Dight chemical vats.

"There must be a bottle here somewhere."

Suddenly beside her shoulder the girl saw a black widow spider crawling through an open ventilator shaft. In horror she backed away quickly. Then she killed it with her shoe.

"I wonder what's on the other side of the ventilator."

An idea came to her. "Maybe Bushy Trott uses spiders to make silk thread the way Mr. Booker does."

Excited, she looked through the ventilator. It was dark beyond, but Nancy found a switch which lighted the inner room. It was filled with glass cases, but she could not see what was in them.

"I must find out if they're spiders that spin silk

thread," she decided. "If so, that will be another bit of evidence against Mr. Dight."

Near the ventilator was a door which apparently led to the room. To Nancy's annoyance it had no knob or visible lock, nor could it be pushed or pulled.

"It must open by means of a secret spring," she reasoned.

With infinite patience Nancy moved her hand over every inch of the panel. Suddenly the door swung inward.

"I must have touched the spring!" she thought gleefully.

Scarcely had the door closed behind her when she heard footsteps outdoors. Evidently the night watchman, attracted by the light she had turned on, had come to investigate. But the man did not come in.

"Doesn't he have a key," Nancy pondered, "or doesn't he suspect an intruder's in here?"

All this while Nancy had continued to explore the inner room of the laboratory. She noticed that the cases contained spiders. But they were not the harmless orb weavers like those at the Booker factory.

"They're deadly black widows but just as useful for thread," Nancy reflected. "Bushy Trott has courage to work with the poisonous things. I wonder what Effie would say to that."

Effie! Nancy suddenly recalled her promise to go back to Pleasant Hedges. She glanced at her watch and was startled to see how late it was.

"I must get a sample of the chemical solution in the other room, and then find my way out," Nancy decided.

Once more she pressed against the secret panel and it swung open. Quietly she returned to the outer room and hunted for an empty container.

"I know!" Nancy chuckled. "Why didn't I think of it before?"

In her pocket were two miniature bottles, part of the March collection. She had intended to offer them to Mr. Dight, but in her haste to leave his office she had forgotten to do so.

Though small, each receptacle was provided with a large stopper. Taking care not to wet her fingers with the chemical, Nancy filled the containers from two different tanks.

Again she heard footsteps outside the building. What should she do? Turn off the light or leave it on?

Nancy decided to leave it on to avoid calling further attention to herself. "But I'd better escape as soon as possible," she thought. Then she remembered that Trott had locked all the doors. Recalling that there was another door inside the spidery, she decided to take a chance on that one.

Again she pressed the secret spring, and the

door opened. As she slid through, Nancy heard the squeal of car brakes outside. Then came the sound of running feet.

In panic Nancy sped to the door at the far end of the spidery. She felt a momentary sense of helplessness when it would not yield, but with an extra tug it opened.

A steep flight of steps led downward. As she groped along Nancy became aware of a cool breeze blowing across her face.

"That's fresh clean air!" she said to herself, trying to be calm. "This cellar must have an outside exit!"

Inching her way, Nancy followed the stream of air. Not far ahead she saw a dim patch of light. Stumbling toward it, she came to the entrance of a low tunnel with a tiny electric bulb above it.

"This must be the way out!" she decided.

Bending over, Nancy crept along. The tunnel was not long. Soon the floor began to slope at a steep angle. In another dozen yards Nancy came to a heavy door with a small barred opening in it. The door was not locked from her side, so she opened it without difficulty. After closing the door which locked itself, she climbed a flight of stone steps to an alley.

"Free!" she congratulated herself. "But what a scare!"

Nancy stood for a moment by the factory wall.

Breathing deeply of the night air, she sought to get her bearings. Some distance away she saw a street lamp and a main thoroughfare. She decided that it must be at the south boundary of the plant.

Nancy started forward, but immediately paused. A man had just entered the alley. He held his head so low, she could not see his face. His manner of walking, however, was familiar.

"That's Bushy Trott!" she thought in panic. "If he catches me here, all of my night's work may be a total loss!"

Frantic, Nancy looked about for a hiding place in the alley. She did not want to go back to the cellar.

"Perhaps he won't notice me behind this gasoline drum!" she thought hopefully.

The alleyway was in deep shadow, lighted only by the far-off street lamp at the entrance. Crouching behind the drum, Nancy waited.

The man came nearer, and passed within a foot of Nancy but did not see her. Trott descended to the cellar passageway. A moment later Nancy heard the dull click of a lock as the heavy door swung shut.

"Lucky I didn't hide down there!" she thought. "Now to get home!"

Out in the street Nancy got her bearings and headed for the convertible. As she stepped inside, the young detective breathed a sigh of relief.

"I really must watch my step," Nancy said to herself.

In a short time she reached her own house. Through an unshaded window in the living room, she could see Hannah Gruen talking excitedly to her father. He was pacing the floor nervously.

"Wonder if they're worried about me," Nancy thought as she unlocked the front door and hurried inside.

"Nancy! Where have you been?" exclaimed Mr. Drew.

Mrs. Gruen was equally relieved. "I've been so worried about you!"

With a great sigh Nancy dropped to the sofa. Now that the strain was over, she realized how utterly exhausted she was.

"I've had a perfectly awful experience," she confessed. "I was locked in the Dight factory."

"Locked in!" her father cried.

"Mr. Dight has a room where he keeps black widow spiders. One of the horrible things was only a few inches from my shoulder. But I'm glad I went there, just the same."

"I shudder to think of your taking such risks to help me, my dear," her father said. "Come have dinner, and tell me everything."

While the housekeeper hurried to reheat Nancy's meal, the young detective removed the tiny bottles of fluid from her pocket and carefully placed them on the table.

"Here's some of the solution from Mr. Dight's private laboratory. It certainly looks as if he has copied Mr. Booker's method of making the beautiful silk thread."

"I'll take this sample to Mr. Booker tomorrow!" the lawyer exclaimed. "If it proves to be the same formula as his, then I can institute proceedings against Mr. Dight."

Nancy related her adventure in detail as she ate, then said she had promised Effie she would return to the March mansion for the night.

"Dad, would you drive me out to Pleasant Hedges?"

"Glad to."

Meanwhile at the March home Effie was growing more and more alarmed because Nancy had failed to arrive. Every time Effie heard a car on the road, she would listen and wait for it to appear, pressing her face against the windowpane and peering out through the dark pines.

"Nancy never broke a promise to me before," she told Mr. March. "She knows I'm scared to stay here at night without her."

"I'm sure something important came up," he replied. "Better stop worrying."

When ten o'clock came he retired. Effie decided that it would be futile to wait longer for Nancy.

Reluctantly she went to her room and prepared for bed.

"What a dark, gloomy night!" the maid observed as she looked out a window. "Not even a moon—"

Her thoughts on the weather ended abruptly. Beneath the window she saw a stealthy, indistinct figure move. Someone was creeping along the high, untrimmed hedge which ran beside the wing of the rambling house!

CHAPTER XI

The Mysterious Letter

EFFIE tried to scream, but no sound came from her throat. She recoiled a step from the window. When the girl regained sufficient courage to look out again, the man was gone.

Terrified, Effie leaped into bed. For a long while she lay absolutely still, the covers pulled up to her ears.

"I locked all the doors and windows before I came to bed," she encouraged herself. "A man couldn't get into this place—or could he?"

A sudden sharp breeze rattled the windows. Overhead timbers groaned.

"Now was that the wind, or was it someone walking across a loose board?" Effie speculated.

The maid could not sleep. She was convinced that the man she had seen outside had slipped into the house.

"Maybe he knows a secret way to get in," Effie

tormented herself. "Maybe he's in the house right now! Oh dear! What was that?"

Distinctly she heard a door down the hall open with a squeak. Then footsteps with measured tread came along the hall.

Effie could bear the suspense no longer. Though frightened half out of her wits, she tiptoed to her bedroom door and opened it a crack.

"Oh, it's you, Mr. March!" she exclaimed in relief, recognizing him in a moment. "I thought it was someone sneaking along the hall!" She told him of the prowling figure outside.

"There's no one in here," he said. Though Mr. March himself had heard suspicious noises, he did not wish to alarm the maid. "You'd better go back to bed, Effie."

"I can't sleep for thinking of Miss Nancy," the girl wailed. "She promised to come back tonight. Oh, I hope nothing has happened to her."

Mr. March tried to reassure Effie. "She probably thought it was too late to phone us."

Satisfied, Effie returned to her bed and immediately dropped into a deep slumber. Mr. March himself felt jittery.

"I wish Nancy *had* stayed here tonight," he muttered. "I'm going upstairs." The elderly man went to get a candle.

Warily he climbed the attic stairs and looked around. There did not appear to be anyone on the third floor. He poked among the various boxes and trunks, but found nothing out of the ordinary.

"Both Effie and I distinctly heard sounds," he kept telling himself.

Finally Mr. March went downstairs and got back into bed. But he could not sleep.

Suddenly the elderly man became aware of a car motor and voices outside. Going to a front window, he was relieved to see Nancy and her father.

Mr. March hurried below to welcome the Drews. Nancy's father stayed only a moment before heading back to his own home.

"I'm sorry to be so late," Nancy apologized. "I was delayed."

Soon she was listening to an account of the strange noises and the prowling figure at Pleasant Hedges.

"But there's no point in investigating further tonight," he finished. "All seems quiet now, and Effie has settled down."

"I'm just sorry I wasn't here earlier," Nancy declared. "I was doing some sleuthing for Dad."

"You must be tired, Nancy," Mr. March said gently. "Get some sleep and we'll tackle this mystery again tomorrow."

Nancy was glad to say good night, and quickly got into bed. She fell asleep almost at once.

As Nancy was finishing a late breakfast the next morning, Mrs. French dropped in to say good-by. "And how is my dear little Susan?" she asked. "I miss taking care of her."

Mr. March smiled at his old friend, who had looked after his granddaughter so lovingly. "Susan and I are going to miss you," he said.

"I'll miss you," she said. "Maybe you can visit us in our new home."

She went upstairs to say good-by to Susan. Mr. March followed.

Nancy decided to go home and work on the Dight mystery. After telling Effie she would be back that afternoon, the young detective left the old mansion.

At home she found Bess and George waiting for her. "You really move in on a mystery!" Bess teased. "We never know whether to look for you here or at the Marches'."

"But I'm still no closer to finding the missing music," Nancy admitted.

"That house keeps its secrets well."

"How about having lunch downtown with Bess and me?" George suggested.

"Fine idea!" Nancy agreed. "I'll tell Hannah I won't be here."

"By the way, how are you making out with Diane?" George asked.

"She gave me several pretty dresses for Susan,"

Nancy replied. Because of the confidential nature of her father's case, she thought it best not to reveal anything she had learned at the Dight factory.

After telling the housekeeper her plans, Nancy stopped at the hall table to look through the mail which had just come. At once she seized a letter from the Jenner Music Publishing Company in Oxford.

As Nancy tore open the envelope, she explained to the girls that she had written to the firm several days before to ask for information about the composer Ben Banks. I'll read it aloud.

" 'Dear Miss Drew,
    We regret that we are unable to provide any of the information you requested concerning Ben Banks, whose songs we publish.
                        Sincerely yours,
                            Milton Jenner' "

"Well, that's a cool answer," George remarked. "What's so secret about the information?"

"I wish I knew," Nancy replied slowly. "I'm going to phone for an appointment."

She looked up the number and dialed it. Nancy was informed that Mr. Jenner never granted appointments by phone. She would have to write for an appointment.

Disappointed, she told this to Bess and George.

"Do you mind waiting while I write a note?" Nancy asked.

"Not at all," Bess replied. "We'll go talk with Hannah."

"And Bess will help herself to some cookies," George teased her cousin.

In the note Nancy stated that there was a matter of vital importance she would like to discuss with Mr. Jenner. She would appreciate talking to him as soon as possible. When Nancy finished the note, she called Bess and George.

"Come with me while I mail this," she suggested. "Then we'll eat. How about you girls going out to Pleasant Hedges with me for the night? Effie ought to have some time off."

"That place is anything but pleasant," Bess remarked. "It gives me the creeps."

"Oh, a ghost or two won't hurt you," George kidded her. "Let's go!"

After a pleasant luncheon, Nancy drove the girls home. "I'll pick you up at four o'clock," she said.

Before going home Nancy did several errands. They included buying supplies for the March household. On impulse Nancy stopped in the leading music store and asked for copies of all the songs composed by Ben Banks.

"There are only three," the clerk told her. "I have both the records and sheet music of 'Song of the Wind' and these other two. They're newer."

"When were they published?"

"Very recently. They came out one right after the other. Ben Banks must be a cool guy to compose three great songs in such a short period of time."

Nancy thought so too. It sounded very suspicious. She listened to the records but did not buy them because Mr. March had no player. She did buy the sheet music, however, and sat down at the store's piano to play the two selections she had not heard before.

"You do all right, miss," the clerk complimented her.

Nancy smiled, paid for the sheet music, and left the shop. Her mind was working fast. She was sure Mr. March had whistled parts of the melodies she had just played. Then a sudden thought struck her.

"If Ben Banks stole them from Fipp March, I wonder if his publisher knows," she mused. "It could explain his giving out no information."

At four o'clock Nancy met Bess and George and drove to the March house. Effie greeted them at the door.

Nancy said to her, "Tonight you go to the movies and then home for the night. We'll stay here."

"Wow!" said Effie in delight, hurrying off to change her clothes.

While Bess and George were starting preparations for supper, Nancy went to find Mr. March. He was trying to seal a crack in the second-floor hall ceiling.

"I have something to show you," she said, holding out the music. "Does this look like your son's work?"

"Now bless you, I wouldn't know!" exclaimed Mr. March, peering at the sheets. "I can't read music."

"I'll sing the melodies to you," Nancy offered.

After hearing them, the elderly man cried out, "Yes, those are Fipp's tunes! I'd like to go into court and face that thief Ben Banks!"

Nancy told him about the letter she had received and the reply she had sent.

"Good," he said. "Those songs belong to the Marches, and I want the world to know it!"

"I wish I could find some definite proof before I meet Mr. Jenner," said Nancy. "Tomorrow I'll hunt for some more."

Supper was a delicious meal, which included a special casserole of beef and vegetables, ice cream and cake. Mr. March was delighted.

"This seems like old times." He chuckled. "It's like one of the family dinner parties we used to have."

Shortly after supper Nancy put Susan to bed.

But the child was not sleepy. She begged for one story after another.

"Tell me about a king," she said.

"Well, once upon a time—"

Nancy's voice trailed off. Susan noticed that her attention was focused on the garden.

"Why don't you go on?" the little girl asked impatiently. "Do you see something?"

Nancy did not reply. Jumping quickly to her feet, she moved closer to the window. The hour was well past nine o'clock and dusk had settled over the garden.

In the gleam of light from the kitchen windows she saw the bushes move. As they parted, the dark, shadowy figure of a man glided forward. Was this the man Effie had seen?

"I'll be back in a minute," Nancy said to Susan.

Without taking time to tell anyone what she intended to do, Nancy hastened outdoors in pursuit of the prowler.

CHAPTER XII

A Surprising Discovery

In the darkness it was not easy for Nancy to distinguish objects, but she dimly saw the back of a man. He disappeared around a corner of the house. By the time she reached the spot, he had vanished.

"Now where did he go so quickly?" she asked herself, perplexed.

She listened for footsteps, but could hear none.

"He must have gone into the house," she speculated excitedly. "But where?"

Cautiously she circled the old mansion, looking at each darkened window for a telltale light. None appeared.

"If that man is in the house, he must know his way around in the dark!" Nancy thought. "I must warn the others."

She hurriedly went inside. Nancy spoke first to Bess and George, who were still in the kitchen.

"There is a prowler around," she said breathlessly. "Will you please post yourselves outdoors and yell if you see him leave the house."

"Where are *you* going?" George asked.

"To the attic."

"Not alone?" Bess quavered.

"I'll get Mr. March."

The elderly man was considerably upset by Nancy's announcement. After making sure that Susan was all right, they tiptoed to the attic door. Quietly Mr. March opened it.

As he did so, creaking sounds came from overhead. This was followed by the same harplike notes Nancy had heard once before.

There was no sign of a light above them. Nancy and Mr. March waited. Complete silence.

The stillness was broken by Susan. Afraid, the child had come into the hall. Seeing the listening figures, she sped toward them, crying.

"What's the matter? Why are you going up to the attic?" she asked in a loud voice.

For a second Nancy was distressed that the child had unwittingly alerted whoever was in the attic. Suddenly it occurred to her that she might put Susan's questions to good use. She said in a loud voice:

"Get into bed, dear, and we'll tell you a story."

She motioned to Mr. March to take the little girl away. Nancy lighted the candle she was holding, and noiselessly stepped to the stairway. She closed the door behind her with a bang.

"If someone is in the attic, I hope he thinks I went the other way," she reflected.

For several minutes she stood still. No light appeared above her. There were no sounds except the murmur of Mr. March's voice as he sought to calm Susan with a story.

Finally Nancy inched her way up the stairway, testing each step for creaky spots before putting her weight on it. Reaching the top step, she held the candle at arm's length. Quickly she scanned the entire attic.

"No one here now," she decided. She sniffed suddenly. "Smoke!"

Nancy's heart leaped wildly. Was the place on fire?

She sniffed again. No, not a fire, but someone had been smoking recently in the attic!

At that instant Mr. March called up sharply, "*Nancy!*"

"Yes?"

"Are you all right?"

"Yes. I didn't find anyone here."

The elderly man started up the stairs. "I had no idea you were going to the attic alone," he said. "I thought you would wait until I could get back."

Before Nancy had a chance to reply, they heard a shout from the garden.

"Bess and George must have seen the man," Nancy cried, hurrying down the steps.

She raced all the way to the front door. Her friends were running through the pine grove toward the main road. Nancy took after them as fast as she could.

The chase ended abruptly a short distance from the road, when they heard a motor start and saw a red tail light disappear around a bend. Their quarry had apparently jumped into a car and driven off!

"If that isn't the worst luck!" George cried. "We almost had him."

"It's a shame," said Nancy. "Did you get a look at him?"

"No, it was too dark," Bess replied. "He seemed to sneak out of nowhere so unexpectedly."

"He was carrying a rolled paper in his right hand," George reported.

"Did he come from the house?" Nancy asked.

"We don't know. All of a sudden there he was, just ahead of us. When George yelled, he started to run."

Mr. March met the girls at the front door. He had wanted to help in the chase, but the excitement had frightened Susan again, and it seemed wiser to stay with her.

It took Nancy a while to quiet the little girl, but soon her eyelids closed and she fell into a sound sleep. Nancy tiptoed to the hall and went downstairs.

In the living room Bess had turned on the radio, to restore her courage so she would dare to stay in the spooky old house. Mr. March suddenly jumped up from his chair.

"They've done it again!" he cried.

"Done what?" Bess asked.

Before he could reply, the music died away. The announcer's voice was clear and crisp. Nancy fully expected to hear the name Ben Banks. Therefore she was startled at what she did hear.

"You have just listened to a new composition by Harry Hall. This completes the program of The Magic Hour. Listen in again tomorrow at the same time—"

Mr. March angrily snapped off the switch.

"I'll do more than listen!" he fumed. "Harry Hall indeed! My son wrote that—every note of it. If I can only scrape together a few dollars, I'll take the case to court."

Then, remembering that he had no evidence to support his case, he sat down utterly dejected. Nancy tried to encourage him.

"Is there anyone besides your family who heard Fipp play the songs? Anyone who might positively identify him as the composer?"

Mr. March shook his head. "There's no one I know of," he admitted. "Mrs. Peabody used to come to the house to hear Fipp play the piano, but she died last year."

"Didn't Fipp have any younger friends?"

"Plenty of them, but they've scattered to the far corners of the earth. I wouldn't know where to find them."

Nancy tried a different approach. "Are you certain that your son never sold any of his tunes?"

"Fipp wouldn't sell his music. He composed it because he loved to. I'm sure he would have told his wife Connie if he had sold any of his songs."

Although she did not suggest it to Mr. March, Nancy was afraid another piece of music had been stolen from the attic that very evening. As the three girls were getting ready for bed, Nancy told her friends about smelling smoke on the third floor.

Then she asked, "Are you sure you saw a rolled paper in the hand of the man we were chasing?"

The girls nodded.

"Do you think it was a sheet of music?" Bess asked.

"I'm afraid so," Nancy replied. "There's no telling how long thieving may have been going on here. Well, if I can't locate the music, perhaps I can find a clue to the thief right in this house."

"How?" George asked.

"I have an idea. We'll try it out in the morning," said Nancy.

Pressed by her friends for an explanation, she revealed her suspicion that there might be a secret entrance to the attic.

"And you think that's how our thief got out?" Bess queried.

"I'm convinced of it. Mr. March and I both heard the floor creak, and I know someone was smoking."

As soon as Effie arrived in the morning to take over the housekeeping duties, Nancy and her friends went outdoors to examine the old mansion for signs of a concealed entrance.

"Hunt for clapboards that can be moved," Nancy directed. "Secret doors alongside real ones, false windows, hidden—"

"That's enough to start with!" George laughed.

The girls separated. They inspected every inch of the foundation and first-floor walls. Nancy spent a long time in the old servants' quarters to see if there might be any kind of a concealed opening into the main part of the house. None of the girls found one.

"There's only one thing left for us to do," said Nancy. "Hide in the bushes tonight and spy on the intruder."

"What do we do in the meantime? Get some sleep?" George asked.

"I propose we go up to the attic and hunt for a hidden entrance," Nancy declared. "We'll have to take a candle. I haven't had a chance to get a new battery for my flashlight."

The three friends trooped to the third floor.

"I once heard rapping sounds up here," said Nancy. "Maybe there's a secret panel that has to be knocked on in order to make it open."

Bess stayed close to Nancy as she began rapping her knuckles against the low walls under the sloping roof.

George decided to look through an old bureau. Remembering that Mr. March needed money, she kept her eyes open for salable articles.

"Here's some beautiful lace," she called out, taking it from the drawer.

"Let's see!" Bess cried.

George held up several dainty pieces. "Old lace is valuable," she declared. "Someone who appreciates beautiful things will pay Mr. March a good price for this lovely work."

"Have you anyone in mind?" Bess asked.

"Yes," George replied. "Madame Paray the dressmaker. Maybe she'll put some of it on a dress for Diane Dight." George grinned.

At that instant Bess screamed, "Oh! Take it away!"

She stood as if transfixed. The girl had backed up toward the wardrobe, and the door had swung open. The long bony fingers of the skeleton had enmeshed themselves in her hair!

Quickly George released its hold. Bess sank shaking onto a trunk.

"See the way that skeleton hangs there with its back against the rear of the wardrobe and the other bony arm half upraised?" Bess pointed out. "Just as if it were beckoning to us to come into the closet!"

"Why, so it does!" Nancy agreed. She moved closer to the wardrobe. "Perhaps Fipp March placed the skeleton that way to convey a message to his family. Possibly there's a secret hiding place—"

"Oh, Nancy, close the door!" Bess urged.

While Bess looked on with disapproval, Nancy began an examination of the massive wardrobe. She had done so before, but this time the young detective paid particular attention to the section underneath the skeleton. Inch by inch she ran her hand over the floor of the big piece of furniture.

"Hold the candle, George," she requested.

The other girl came closer.

"I can feel something with my fingers!" Nancy said in an excited voice. "It's a tiny knob!" she cried. "Girls, I've found a secret compartment!"

Again and again she tugged, trying to pull it up. The wood had swollen from dampness and the lid was stuck fast.

"Let me try my luck!" George urged impatiently.

Before she could test her strength, Effie appeared at the head of the stairs.

"Miss Nancy, there's a man downstairs to see you," she announced.

"To see me? I didn't think anyone knew I was here."

"Mrs. Gruen sent him," Effie explained. "And he says he can't wait long."

"What's his name?"

"Mr. Jenner."

The publisher of Ben Banks' music!

CHAPTER XIII

An Unpleasant Caller

THE unexpected appearance of the music publisher at the March home surprised Nancy. She
asked Bess and George if they wanted to continue
working on the secret compartment in the cabi-
net, or go downstairs with her.

"Maybe we can find some evidence against Mr.
Jenner while you're talking with him," George
suggested, tugging at the knob in the floor of the
wardrobe.

Nancy hurried down the stairs to meet the song
publisher. She was sorry that Mr. March had gone
to town and could not meet him.

"But perhaps it's just as well that he isn't here,"
she reasoned. "The poor man gets so excited
thinking of his son's music having been stolen
that he might say something to harm his own
chances."

Mr. Jenner proved to be an unpleasant-looking man with a brisk manner.

"I haven't much time to spend here," he said snappily. "Are you Miss Nancy Drew?"

"I am," the young detective replied calmly.

Mr. Jenner did not waste words. He spoke of the letters which she had sent to him. "Although you didn't say anything definite, you hinted at an accusation."

"What do you know about Mr. Banks?" Nancy began.

"Very little. Most of our contact has been through correspondence."

"What can you tell me about a composer named Harry Hall?" Nancy asked. She had a hunch that he, too, published through Jenner.

"He's another of my songwriters—a very talented person. I've never met him. He always sends his work in by mail."

"Can you vouch for his honesty?"

"What is this, a quiz program?" the publisher demanded, getting red in the face. "I'll admit I don't know much about either of the men, but their music is equal to the best that is being put out today."

"And for good reason, perhaps."

"What do you mean? Don't tell me you think someone else wrote it!"

"Maybe you should make sure no one else did," Nancy replied, "before you publish it."

"Tell me who has been making such insinuations?" the man snapped.

"I thought I'd give you an opportunity to explain what you know about the matter," Nancy replied.

"I've nothing to explain! I publish the music in good faith. I'm satisfied that the men with whom I deal are the composers of the songs they submit to me."

"And are you prepared to prove it?"

"Certainly I am," Mr. Jenner returned wrathfully. He glanced at his watch. "I made a special trip here to see you, and my valuable time has been wasted."

"You may not think so later."

"What are your reasons for believing that Banks and Hall may be plagiarists?"

"I can't tell you at this moment," Nancy responded. "I do suggest that you buy no more music from either of those men until the matter of the rightful composer has been straightened out."

"What is the name of the person you claim wrote the music?"

"I can't tell you."

"Well, it doesn't worry me in the least," the publisher retorted. "Stupid of me to waste so much time coming here."

Abruptly Mr. Jenner left the house. With min-gled feelings of annoyance and contempt, Nancy watched him drive away.

"Has your caller left so soon?" Bess questioned when Nancy returned to the attic. "We haven't opened the secret compartment yet."

"When we do, I hope it will contain something I can use against Mr. Jenner," said Nancy, and relayed the man's remarks.

Bess and George were incensed. "All I can say is that he'd better look out!" George exclaimed, her eyes blazing.

"Well, after all, I do need evidence." Nancy sighed. "Come on. Let's get at this compartment again."

Nancy gave the knob a quick jerk sideways. A little door pulled up, revealing a recess below.

"It's open!" she cried in delight. "Let's hope Fipp's songs are here!"

Excitedly Nancy thrust her hand into the hole. "Papers!" she exclaimed.

Quickly she pulled out a handful. It was diffi-cult to look at them by candlelight, so the girls took everything out of its hiding place and carried the contents to one of the bedrooms. Mr. March had returned and eagerly helped Nancy look through the mass of old letters. Bess and George began sorting the other papers.

Suddenly Bess cried out, "Here's a piece of original music! It says 'by Fipp March. Based on a melody composed by his grandmother.' "

The group stared at the double sheet.

"Thieves didn't get this, thank goodness!" the elderly man muttered. "I'd like to hear it. Will you play it, Nancy?"

Everyone went downstairs to the music room. Nancy did the best she could on the old piano, while Bess and George hummed the melody.

"It's lovely," Bess said dreamily.

"It would be a hit if it were published," George declared.

"My father knows a reputable music publisher," Nancy said. "Maybe he would buy it."

"Take it home with you," Mr. March urged, "and send it to him."

She had lunch with Mr. Drew and Hannah Gruen, then played the selection for them on her own piano. Both shared her enthusiasm for the lovely music, and declared that it was the equal of the best popular songs on the market.

"I can't make rash promises, but I believe Mr. Hawkins will buy the song," Mr. Drew told his daughter. "I'll take the music to him this afternoon. He's a good friend and a client as well, and we may get some excellent results."

Satisfied that her father would do what he could for Mr. March, Nancy now told him of her plan to try capturing the intruder at Pleasant Hedges.

"I'm sure he's getting in by some secret entrance. But I can't locate it. So tonight we girls plan to watch for him if possible."

"Promise me you'll all use utmost caution," Mr. Drew said.

"All right, Dad. And now tell me about your case. Has the chemical fluid I brought been analyzed yet?" Nancy asked.

"Mr. Booker is having his chief chemist examine the solution and compare it with preparations used in his own plant. So far I've received no report."

"I wish they'd hurry," Nancy said impatiently.

"If you want some action, why not see Mr. Dight again?" her father teased. "He probably was annoyed about the way you disappeared while on the factory grounds."

Nancy made a grimace. "Do you think he found out I was in the lab?"

"Mr. Dight is thorough in his methods. I shouldn't be surprised if he has called in several experts to take fingerprints and solve the riddle of the light you turned on in the laboratory."

"Fingerprints!" Nancy gasped. "Why, I left them everywhere—in the lab, in the spidery, even the tunnel!"

"Then I advise you to steer clear of Mr. Dight unless you're looking for trouble."

"That's just it," Nancy replied with a little

moan. "I'll have to see him. Mr. Dight still has those valuable old bottles belonging to Mr. March. If I don't go back for them, he'll be doubly suspicious. He may even move his secret lab before you can prosecute."

The more Nancy thought of interviewing Mr. Dight, the more she dreaded it. On second thought, though, she doubted that the man had looked for fingerprints.

"Still there's no telling what he found out," she reflected.

Despite her concern, late that afternoon Nancy drove to the factory grounds. With no outward display of nervousness, she greeted Miss Jones, the private secretary.

"May I see Mr. Dight, please?" she requested.

The secretary, formerly so friendly, gazed at the caller without smiling.

"Yes, Mr. Dight very much wants to talk to you, Miss Drew," she replied with emphasis.

CHAPTER XIV

Warning

WITH sinking heart Nancy realized she must play her part convincingly if she expected to keep out of trouble.

"Your sudden disappearance from Mr. Dight's office the other day disturbed him very much," Miss Jones continued.

Nancy pretended not to understand. "My disappearance? Why, didn't Mr. Dight think that when I left his office I was going home?"

"Apparently he didn't. He thought you went off somewhere in the factory."

"Well, no wonder you were concerned!"

"I'll tell Mr. Dight you're here," the young woman said, rising.

In a moment she returned to say that he would see Nancy in his private office. The factory owner sat at his desk, writing. For several seconds he kept on, paying no attention to his young visitor. Finally he looked up.

"Well?" he barked, trying to place Nancy on the defensive. "Did you learn what you were sent here for?"

Nancy knew that Mr. Dight suspected she had been assigned by someone, perhaps her father, to spy on him, but she pretended otherwise.

"Oh, you mean about the bottles?" she said brightly. "I'm sorry I ran off the way I did, but I saw someone in the courtyard I thought I knew. Then it was so late I decided to go on home."

Lawrence Dight gazed quizzically at Nancy.

"And did you go directly home from here?" he questioned sharply.

Nancy was not to be trapped so easily. "Well, you know how it is." She laughed. "I didn't mean to worry anyone, but I stopped to see some friends. I'll confess I didn't get home until rather late. Our housekeeper was quite upset."

"I can imagine," replied Mr. Dight.

The man believed Nancy's story. She figured he had decided that the light in the laboratory must have been left on by one of the workmen in the plant. Bushy Trott had found nothing out of order. He had apparently not even seen the black widow Nancy had killed.

Leaning back in his swivel chair, Mr. Dight

suddenly relaxed. In a friendly tone he began to discuss Mr. March's collection of bottles.

"I've taken quite a fancy to some of that glassware. Now if you'll name your price, young lady, perhaps we can do business."

"The blue bottle was intended as a gift."

"I'll buy the others. Suppose I offer you thirty-five dollars for the entire collection?"

Nancy's face fell. She had expected Mr. Dight to make a low offer, but certainly not one under a hundred dollars.

"Only thirty-five?" she asked. "Oh, I couldn't sell them for that."

"I might make it fifty," Mr. Dight said. "You're a friend of Diane's, so I'll throw in the extra fifteen for good measure."

Nancy arose, glad of an excuse to withdraw in good grace.

"I couldn't think of letting friendship influence me in this transaction, Mr. Dight, "because I'm selling the bottles for someone else. I don't believe the person would be willing to part with them for thirty-five dollars."

"I'll pay you fifty, but not a cent more."

"I'll find out if that's satisfactory," Nancy said, standing firm. She had already decided to consult Mr. Faber the antique dealer. "May I have the bottles, please?"

Obviously unwilling to let the fine collection

out of his possession, Mr. Dight raised his price another ten dollars. When Nancy would not sell them, he reluctantly returned the box of glassware.

Nancy gave a sigh of relief as she got into her car. She hoped never to have to face Lawrence Dight again!

She drove directly to Mr. Faber's shop, and carried the glassware into the quaint little place. The owner was there.

"Well, well," he said. "And what have you brought me this time?"

"Some old bottles. I'd like you to tell me what they're worth."

As Nancy lined them up on the counter, Mr. Faber's blue eyes began to sparkle.

"These bottles are old and fine!" he exclaimed, appraising them at a glance. "I'll pay you a very good price for them."

"Friendship mustn't enter into this," Nancy cautioned him. "Tell me frankly, are the bottles worth more than fifty dollars?"

"I'll pay you double that amount gladly! If you're in no hurry for the money, perhaps I can sell them to a collector who will pay an even higher price."

"The bottles are yours to do with as you wish," Nancy decided instantly. "Perhaps, though, you'd better write a check now for a hundred dollars to

Mr. Philip March. Let me know if you manage to sell them for more later."

"You are always busy helping someone." Mr. Faber beamed at the girl as he handed her the check.

At home Nancy found a telegram awaiting her. It was from Mr. Jenner, the music publisher.

The message both disappointed and annoyed her. Curtly the man informed her that she had made a great mistake in assuming the songs he had published had been stolen.

"Further accusations will lead to a libel suit," Nancy was warned. "Advise you pursue matter no further. Otherwise expect immediate action against you."

Nancy was not fooled by the threat.

"He's frightened and is just trying to scare me," she thought. "Mr. Jenner, Ben Banks, and Harry Hall must be closely associated. I *must* find some proof that Fipp wrote those songs—and soon!"

Bess and George had decided to go back to Pleasant Hedges for the night, so the three girls drove out there after an early supper. They found Mr. March following his usual custom of relating stories to his little grandchild.

When Susan had been tucked in, Nancy told him of her plan to watch the house from outside that evening, hoping to catch the mysterious intruder.

Mr. March was concerned. "I don't know that I should let you do this," he said. "It's very risky."

"Three of us girls ought to be able to handle one man!" George boasted.

Nancy assured the owner of Pleasant Hedges that they would take no unnecessary chances. She had suggested that the three of them wear dark dresses and cover their hair with black kerchiefs. When they left the house and stealthily took the separate posts which Nancy had assigned, they seemed to be only ghostly shadows.

Within the house, life went on in the usual routine. Effie cleared away the supper dishes and went upstairs. Mr. March seated himself in the living room to listen to the radio for clues to any songs stolen from his son. Finally he turned off the radio, put out the light, and climbed the stairs to the second floor.

Nancy and the other girls shifted their positions in the darkness outside. There had been no sign of a trespasser.

It had been decided that if no one appeared by dawn, the chances were that nobody would. Then the three girls were to give up the watch.

From somewhere in the old mansion a clock began to strike, breaking the stillness of the night. Nancy, posted near the old servants' quarters, counted eleven.

From a distance came another sound. Some-

Nancy was not fooled by the threat

thing was stirring. Nancy stood erect, listening intently.

She was puzzled. One moment she thought she heard a soft padding, as if someone were sneaking among the pine trees toward the house. The next minute she was sure light footsteps were approaching from the front of the mansion.

"Maybe the thief has an accomplice," she said to herself.

There was no doubt of it. Two figures were coming nearer and nearer. Nancy held her breath!

CHAPTER XV

Wallpaper Clue

As Nancy waited, the two shadowy forms crept closer. The one coming across the lawn appeared first. Then suddenly the voice of the other cut the air from among the trees.

"Nancy! Where are you?"

Mr. March!

His ill-timed call from the pine grove served as a warning to the intruder. Instantly he turned and fled.

Nancy dashed from her hiding place. As she pursued the running figure, the young detective shouted to her friends to join in the chase.

They came quickly, but the race was futile. The night swallowed up the stranger. As the discouraged girls returned to the house, Nancy explained what had happened.

George was annoyed. "It's bad enough to have

missed capturing the thief, but now he's been warned that we're looking for him."

"We've probably missed our chance, too, of finding out how he gets into the house," added Nancy in disappointment.

"Oh, why did Mr. March have to pick out just that moment to look for us?" Bess complained.

"I suppose he meant well," said Nancy.

The elderly man was apologetic over his untimely appearance. He had grown uneasy about the girls, he explained, and had come outside to make sure they were all right. When he could find no one, he had become fearful that something had happened to them, and had called out, unaware of the nearness of the intruder.

It was agreed that the mysterious stranger certainly would not return that night, so the girls went to bed. Upon awakening the next morning, Nancy heard faint music from a distance.

"Mr. March has the radio on early," she thought.

When Nancy reached the dining room, she found him already at the breakfast table with Susan. But neither of them was eating. They were listening to a man singing.

"One of my Daddy's pieces, Nancy!" cried the little girl.

As Nancy listened, she realized this composition was somewhat different from the others Mr.

March attributed to his son. It was a beautiful love song in waltz time. Three words caught the girl's attention. "My heart's desire—"

"Where have I heard that phrase before in connection with this mystery?" she mused.

For nearly an hour the melody continued to haunt her. Then suddenly she knew why. Running to Mr. March, she exclaimed:

"I believe you were right in the first place about the clue to the missing music."

"How's that?"

"Why, those letters written by your son to his wife! The words 'My heart's desire' appear in one of them!"

"So they do," the elderly man agreed.

Nancy was eager to read the love letters again. Since they were still at her own home, she decided to go there at once.

But before Nancy could leave, Susan called her upstairs to admire the child's "dress up" costume. Holding up a trailing skirt with one hand, she flourished a silk parasol in the other.

"I found these in a hall closet. Let's go down and show Grandpa!" Susan said eagerly. "Do I look like a real grown-up lady now?"

"Those high-heeled shoes certainly make you seem taller." Nancy smiled. "Watch out, or you'll trip!"

As they started down the stairway, the child

stumbled on the steps. Nancy, who was only a few steps behind, grabbed Susan just in time. But the sharp-pointed parasol got out of control and tore a jagged hole in the wallpaper. It revealed several bars of music.

"Oh, I didn't mean to do it!" Susan cried in dismay. "What will Grandpa say?"

"It wasn't your fault," Nancy assured her. "Fortunately you weren't hurt. And you've uncovered a clue!" she exclaimed.

Excitedly Nancy examined the torn place. Several tiny bars of music were painted on the wall!

Nancy summoned Mr. March to the stairway. At first he thought she was calling attention to the costume, but when the elderly man saw the music notes, he too became excited.

"Maybe it's part of one of our old family songs!" he exclaimed. "I'd like to know if there's any more of it here. Let's tear off the paper!" Mr. March urged. "It's too faded to worry about, anyway."

Inch by inch, with the help of Nancy, Bess, and George, he removed a large area of the wall covering. It was slow, tedious work, but at last they were successful. Gradually a charming, old fashioned scene was revealed of a woman seated at a piano and a man beside her singing.

The last bit of paper to come off partially covered the music rack of the piano. Someone had sketched in a sheet of music, the notes of which had first drawn Nancy's attention. Printed in tiny lettering was the composer's name, a member of the March family.

Nancy hummed the pictured notes. The tune was indeed one which Fipp March had elaborated upon, and was a current "hit."

"Now we have real proof that Ben Banks is an impostor! This is one of the melodies he claims as his!" Mr. March exclaimed.

"Would a court accept such evidence?" George asked.

"I think it would," Nancy said soberly. "Of course it might not be necessary to go to such lengths. If Mr. Jenner knows we have a case against him, he'll probably prefer to settle matters without a lawsuit. If you wish, Mr. March, I'll see the publisher."

"Yes, do that," he urged.

Nancy asked Bess and George if they would accompany her to Mr. Jenner's office in Oxford, a town several miles from River Heights. The girls were eager to go, and suggested starting at once. An hour later, they arrived at their destination, a dingy brick structure.

"This isn't very inviting," said Bess as they entered.

From an upstairs room came the strains of a swing band. In another section of the building someone was picking out a few notes on a piano.

"Listen!" Nancy cried suddenly.

"I don't hear anything except that loud music," George declared. "The tune is catchy but all those discords!"

"The person at the piano is playing one of Fipp March's songs!" Nancy said.

The girls moved nearer to the closed door. Soon the piano playing ceased abruptly. After waiting a moment, the callers went along the hall until they came to a door which bore the name of the music publisher. Nancy and her friends entered.

They found themselves in an untidy little room. A desk was piled high with papers, books, and stacks of music. A girl sat at a typewriter. She chewed gum to the rhythm of her typing and did not look up for a long while.

"Well?" she inquired at last.

"May we see Mr. Jenner, please?" Nancy requested politely.

The girl looked her over from head to toe.

"If you have music to sell, you've come to the wrong place. Mr. Jenner isn't buying from amateurs."

"I have nothing to sell," Nancy replied. "Please give my name to your employer."

She removed a card from her purse. The office girl accepted it with a shrug and vanished into an inner room. She did not return for several minutes. Then her message was crisp and to the point.

"Mr. Jenner isn't seeing anybody today except one of his composers. And he said to tell you it wouldn't do any good to come back, either!"

"I see," said Nancy. Flushing slightly, she turned away.

"I was afraid this might happen," she declared as the girls paused in the hall.

"I feel like going back in there and demanding an interview!" George said.

"Let your father handle that horrid man," Bess pleaded.

Determined not to go home without finding out something, Nancy paused again. Then she walked down the corridor where she suspected Mr. Jenner's private office was located. Through an open transom came voices.

"Ben, we're in a tight spot," they heard the music publisher say. "That Drew girl has just left here. Maybe she *has* found some proof."

"Impossible!" replied the other voice.

"Just the same, it may be well to call off your scheduled public appearances and lie low for a while. We can't take chances."

Nancy and her friends strained to hear more. The voices dropped, however, and the girls could not make out another word.

"Mr. Jenner must be talking to Ben Banks!"

Nancy whispered excitedly. "Oh, I wish we could learn more about that fellow!"

"Maybe we can," George said in her friend's ear. "Why not stay around here until he comes out of the office?"

"And then follow him!" Nancy added. "You girls wait outside the building. I'll watch this door."

Bess and George immediately tiptoed down the hallway and vanished. Nancy looked about for a hiding place. The best one she could find was a little niche near the stairway.

Twenty minutes elapsed. At the end of that time the door of Mr. Jenner's office opened. Out stepped a lean, long-haired man of early middle age. He had a roll of music under his arm. Nancy was convinced that he must be Ben Banks.

Waiting until he had rounded the corner, she followed him. At the street entrance she spotted Bess and George standing in a shadowy doorway. With a nod of her head she signaled to them.

The cousins immediately started off in pursuit of Ben Banks. Nancy waited until she was certain her movements would not arouse the songwriter's suspicions. Then she hastened after her friends and caught up with them.

The man walked rapidly. Of one thing Nancy was certain: this thin man was not the strange intruder at the March homestead. The prowler was heavy-set.

Without once glancing back, Banks walked on until he came to a small hotel, the Millette. Entering, he went directly to the desk.

Nancy, Bess, and George stood in the lobby. They heard the man say to the desk clerk:

"My key, please."

"Yes, Mr. Dight," the other replied, handing it to him.

"Dight!" Nancy almost exclaimed aloud.

CHAPTER XVI

Poetic Hint

NANCY and her friends wondered if they had heard correctly. The name of the man they thought was Ben Banks was Dight! To make sure of this, the girls waited until the man had gone up in the elevator. Then they went to the desk.

"Is Mr. Banks registered here?" Nancy asked, smiling at the clerk.

"You mean the composer? Yes, but he uses his own name of Horace Dight. I'm sorry, but Mr. Dight can't see you now. He left word that he didn't want to be disturbed."

The girls left the hotel. On the way back to River Heights, they discussed the new developments in the mystery.

"Do you suppose Mr. Dight is related to Diane's family?" Bess asked.

"This so-called Ben Banks may very well be a

relative," Nancy agreed. "I'll make it my business to find out. If he is, what a tangle this mystery is becoming!"

In the light of the day's discovery, Mr. Drew's case took on new significance. Nancy was eager to get home and talk to her father. She had been in the house only fifteen minutes before he came in.

Nancy asked, "How are things going in the Dight case?"

"Not good for him. Mr. Booker has just informed me that his chemist has analyzed the bottles of fluid you obtained from the Dight factory."

"With what result, Dad?"

"The solutions are the same as those used in the Booker plant to toughen the spider thread."

"Then Lawrence Dight did steal the formula —or rather, hired Bushy Trott to do it!"

"It appears that way. I've decided to prosecute Dight as soon as I can prepare my case."

Nancy then told her father what she had learned about Ben Banks, and the fact that the man's real name was Horace Dight.

"Affairs *are* getting complicated," the lawyer mused.

"I certainly need your advice," Nancy said. "Can you find out anything about Horace Dight?"

"Let me check my files at the office to see if I have anything on him," Mr. Drew offered.

A quick call to his secretary revealed that Lawrence Dight did indeed have a second cousin named Horace.

"You're a really thorough investigator," Nancy remarked with a smile.

"Well, you never know when some small detail about a man's background may prove very useful," Carson Drew replied. "In this case, all I have to go on is the fact that this cousin Horace is a loafer about the same age as Lawrence Dight."

"Where do we go from here?" Nancy wondered. "Ben Banks learned from Mr. Jenner that a certain Nancy Drew knows something about him and wants to know more. He may mention my name to the River Heights Dight family."

"I never thought of that!" exclaimed Mr. Drew. "Maybe I'd better hold up the proceedings against Lawrence Dight until you clear up the March case. And have you found any more of Fipp's songs?"

Nancy shook her head.

"I certainly hope you can," her father said. "Mr. Hawkins has purchased that song you brought me."

"Wonderful!" Nancy exclaimed.

"I received a letter from Hawkins this morning. He liked Fipp March's song very much, and he wants more like it."

"If only I could supply some! So far I haven't

been able to find another piece, Dad. But I believe I have a good clue this time."

She told her father about hearing a tune on the radio which Mr. March believed to be Fipp's and which contained the phrase "My heart's desire."

"I recall reading those words in one of the letters Fipp March wrote to his wife," Nancy explained. "I believe the clue to the missing music —if there's any that hasn't been stolen—may be in those letters after all. Suppose I get them—"

"You'd better pack some clothes and slip away from here," her father advised. "If the Dight cousins suspect you're after them, I'd feel better if they don't know for sure where to find you."

"I see what you mean," Nancy agreed and paused a moment. "The March mansion will serve that purpose. And there's so much at the house I want to investigate. I'll leave now and take the letters with me."

"Good! I'll drive out there if I have anything to report before I hear from you."

Nancy was sorry to leave her father so soon, but he wanted her to get back to Pleasant Hedges while it was still daylight. She had had so much to talk to him about that she had forgotten completely to tell him of the appearance of the strange intruder at the March home.

Upon reaching the old mansion, Nancy immediately sought out Mr. March. She told him that her father's client had bought Fipp's song.

"That's marvelous! Now my son and the March family will have recognition at last. Nancy, I never can repay you for what you've done!"

"Mr. Hawkins would like more songs." Nancy smiled. "I'm going to search harder than ever for them now. Here are your son's letters. Let's look through them for clues."

For some time the elderly man and his guest read without saying a word.

Then suddenly Nancy cried out, "Here's what I was looking for! Listen to this!"

Nancy read from one of Fipp March's letters to his wife:

> " 'No love more true than mine,
>   I would protect thee every day.
>   Among old things and fine,
>   I put my heart's desire away.' "

"It's a pretty verse," said Mr. March. "But as to its being a clue—"

Nancy gave her interpretation of the words. "Your son wanted to provide for his wife always. He put the song with the words 'My heart's desire' among some fine old things. She was to find the music and sell it if the need arose."

"I see. And you think he meant he hid it somewhere in our attic?"

"Perhaps," Nancy replied. "Let's see if we can find another clue among these letters. I have a hunch the key to the mystery is right here."

A very few minutes later Nancy came across a lovely verse. "I believe I've found it!" she exclaimed excitedly. She read it aloud:

> " 'Long-forgotten man,
>   My secret you hide,
>   Reveal it to my love,
>   That comfort may abide.' "

"That means less to me than the other verse," declared Mr. March. "What do you make of it?"

" 'Long-forgotten man' must be the skeleton! He guards a secret which, when found, will bring comfort to your son's family!"

"Maybe," the elderly man agreed. "But you've already found the secret drawer in the wardrobe. There was only one song in it."

Despite this, Nancy was hopeful about the skeleton clue. She insisted upon going to the attic at once for a further investigation of the skeleton and the wardrobe. Mr. March followed her, carrying a lighted candle.

"I can't stand many more disappointments," he said in a gloomy tone. "Each time I think something surely will come of the search, only failure has been the result. I haven't enough money to start suit against Ben Banks or Harry Hall."

"I have a hunch that this time we're going to be successful!" Nancy declared.

As soon as they reached the attic, Nancy went to the old wardrobe and gingerly opened the door. This time she had a very different impression of the skeleton. It did not seem sinister to her; in fact, she could almost imagine it was trying to be friendly.

"Maybe that's just because we've met so often!" she thought with a smile. "Or else it could hold a very vital clue to good fortune for Mr. March and Susan."

Carefully she removed the bony skeleton from the hook. Where its head had hung, a tiny hole could be seen on the back wall of the wardrobe!

"Perhaps this means something!" she said with increasing hope.

A long, round curtain rod lay on the floor. She picked it up and carefully ran one end through the circular hole in the wardrobe. The rod touched no wall or object beyond.

Puzzled, Nancy removed the rod and peered through the tiny hole. She could see nothing—not even a glimmer of light.

"That's odd," she said to Mr. March and stepped aside so he could take a look.

"Wh–what do you suppose—?" the elderly man gasped.

"I always assumed," Nancy said, "that this

wardrobe stood against an outside wall of the attic."

"I did myself," Mr. March added, still mystified.

"There must be a room or niche beyond! Otherwise we'd see daylight!"

"You're right, my dear." Mr. March shook his head. He laughed gently and added, "To think I've lived here all these years without discovering this! You've shown me now that I must not take anything for granted."

Thrilled by her discovery, Nancy said she would run downstairs and out-of-doors to take a look at the architecture of the house. When she inspected the exterior of the mansion critically, she could see that a small section of the main house connected with the roof over the old servants' quarters.

"There must be a secret room up there," Nancy thought excitedly.

CHAPTER XVII

The Hidden Room

DARTING into the house, Nancy hurried back to the attic.

"Learn anything?" Mr. March asked.

"Oh yes." Breathlessly she told him of her find.

"I never knew of any hidden room!" he exclaimed. "But come to think of it, Fipp would disappear for hours at a time. We didn't know where he was and he never told us anything, so we didn't ask."

"Perhaps your son found the room and kept it a secret for his music! Let's move the wardrobe and investigate."

Nancy and Mr. March found it was too heavy for them to budge, so Nancy went off to summon Effie from her supper preparations.

"We need a strong pusher," she told the maid.

Effie grinned. "I can oblige," she said. "What's on your mind?"

"Furniture moving."

By working together the three finally succeeded in shifting the massive oak wardrobe a few more inches. Susan, who had come upstairs, watched with deep interest.

Suddenly she clapped her hands and began to dance around excitedly.

"There it is! A door with a peephole in the wall!"

"Sure's you're born, it is!" Effie agreed, staring in astonishment. "I wouldn't have believed it. Yet there seems to be all kinds of funny things going on around here."

The door was a crude, homemade affair, evidently built by someone with little skill in carpentry or craftsmanship.

"Fipp must have put that in himself, the rascal!" Mr. March chuckled. "He was always tinkering."

Nancy unbolted the door and pushed with all her strength. It refused to give.

"That's queer," said Mr. March. "Let me try it."

He had no better success than Nancy. Effie also tried but to no avail.

"It must be bolted on the other side," she said. "In that case we'll never be able to get in."

Many thoughts flashed through Nancy's mind. The strange musical notes and the rapping sounds she had heard must have come from beyond this locked door. With no apparent opening to the place from the old servants' quarters, how did anyone get inside?

Effie whispered hoarsely, "I'll bet there's a ghost beyond there! Please leave it alone. Don't let it out! No telling what it'll do to us!"

The remark brought Nancy back to reality. She was provoked that the maid had spoken, for her statement had frightened Susan. The child clung to Nancy.

"Effie, go downstairs and take Susan with you," Nancy said, rather severely. "There are no such things as ghosts and you know it. Mr. March and I will continue the work alone."

The maid, somewhat embarrassed, took the child by the hand and went to the second floor. Although Nancy had declared there could not be a ghost beyond the locked door, she was apprehensive as to what they might find.

"Shall we break the door down?" she asked Mr. March.

He nodded.

Together they pushed against the door. Suddenly there was a splintering sound, and the barricade gave way.

Nancy and Mr. March fell forward. There was no floor beyond the door. Man and girl pitched into space!

Mr. March and Nancy pitched into space!

For a second Nancy thought she had hurtled to the outdoors. But suddenly, with Mr. March beside her, she crashed onto something hard.

The two, their breath knocked from them, lay still for a few moments. Then Nancy roused herself.

"Are you all right?" she asked, getting up and helping Mr. March to rise.

"Yes," he panted. "Guess we missed some steps."

The candlelight was still visible at a distance, but most of its beam was cut off by the massive wardrobe. As Nancy's eyes became accustomed to the dimness, she groped toward the doorway of the attic to retrieve the light.

She found three steps leading from the secret room to the attic and climbed up. Effie was standing there, trembling.

"I heard a crash—" she began.

"Everything's all right," Nancy assured her. "Mr. March and I had a fall, but we weren't hurt —just a few bruises."

"Thank goodness!" Effie cried. "Oh my, you could have killed yourselves! Did you find anything?"

"Not yet. We'll let you know as soon as we do."

Effie went downstairs again. Nancy got the candle and returned to the secret room. Her first thought was to find out how the person who had bolted the door from the inner side had gained access to the room. Nothing showed up until she looked above her.

"A skylight!" she said aloud, and played the candle on the low arched ceiling. "Look, Mr. March, it has been entirely covered with a large black cloth."

"A person could step in and out of that window easily," Mr. March remarked. "The fellow put the dark cloth over it to keep anyone from seeing a light in here. And come to think of it, Fipp often went to his bedroom early. Probably he came up here instead of going to bed."

Nancy was not entirely sure the elderly man was correct in his surmise about the skylight being the entrance. There was no evidence outdoors that an intruder could possibly gain access to the steep roof without a long ladder.

"And that certainly would have been noticed," Nancy thought.

She and Mr. March searched for another opening, but were unable to find one. Nancy had to conclude that Mr. March's theory probably was correct, yet a strong hunch told her it was not.

"Now let's look for Fipp's music," said Mr. March.

The only pieces of furniture in the room were a small antique piano-desk and a drawerless table.

Nancy inquired if Mr. March had ever seen them before.

"Yes, long ago," he replied. "But I seem to recall that they stood along a wall in the attic at that time."

Nancy began to examine the unusual piano-desk, feeling that if Fipp's music were hidden any place, it would be there. Lightly she struck a few of the yellowed keys, and then her heart sank.

"These harplike notes are the very ones I heard the other day!" she exclaimed.

"Are you sure?" Mr. March asked.

"Positive."

To herself Nancy said, "I'm afraid the intruder knew the secret of this old attic and has found all the music. One by one the songs will be published, and there won't be a scrap of evidence to bring suit against the thief! The one clue we found under the wallpaper on the staircase won't help us much."

Mr. March shared her feeling of discouragement as they pulled out one drawer after another of the piano-desk. They contained nothing.

"Perhaps there's a secret drawer under the keys," said Nancy, taking heart suddenly. "Those musical notes I heard may be part of some special combination that's used to open a hidden compartment."

"Didn't you say you heard rapping sounds as

well?" Mr. March reminded her. "Maybe you have to rap on something while you strike the notes. But what's the use of bothering if all the music is gone?"

"We don't *know* that all of it is gone," Nancy told the elderly man. "Maybe the thief was only experimenting, just as we are, and didn't find the combination."

Nancy tried to imitate the sounds exactly as she had heard them. Again and again she played the musical notes, while rapping first on one part, then another of the wooden framework with her free hand.

She was just about to give up when a drawer shot out just above the piano keys.

CHAPTER XVIII

Trapped

"THERE'S nothing in the secret drawer!" Mr. March groaned in disappointment. "The thief got here first and took it all!"

"Here's a card with writing on it," said Nancy, reaching in and taking out the message. "Maybe it gives further directions."

"Read it to me," Mr. March directed.

Nancy was so excited that the words tumbled from her mouth. Here, in telltale handwriting, was a splendid clue to the man who had stolen the March songs and to the person who had them published as his own original compositions! Mr. March requested that the girl repeat it.

" 'Riggin,
    Can't you find another good song?
                  D.' "

" 'D' for Dight, you think?" Mr. March asked.

"I'm sure of it," Nancy replied, elated at the discovery. "But who can Riggin be? Whoever he is he must have dropped this card when he was searching for the songs."

At that instant Effie appeared in the doorway. "Isn't anybody going to eat supper? It'll be stone-cold pretty soon."

The maid's words brought the searchers back to reality.

"Why, yes, Effie. We'll be right down," Mr. March said.

"You two look awful funny. Did something happen?" Effie inquired.

"We've had a surprise, that's all," Nancy answered. "But we didn't find what we'd hoped to."

Before leaving the secret room, Mr. March decided to nail up the skylight so the intruder could not get in again. He called to Effie to bring hammer and nails from his toolbox in the basement.

"But it's like locking the barn door after the horse has been stolen," he said dolefully.

"Maybe not," said Nancy, a new thought coming to her. "You know the intruder hasn't been back since we frightened him away. Whatever he wanted hasn't been taken yet."

"True enough," the elderly man agreed. "There's still a ray of hope."

"Just where to look next puzzles me," said

Nancy. "I'd like to sit down quietly and think things out."

Effie returned with hammer and nails. The skylight was securely fastened. Then they all went downstairs.

During supper no mention was made of the secret room. Susan was eating with her grandfather and Nancy, and they did not want to excite the child. It was not until the little girl had gone to the kitchen after the meal to talk to Effie that Mr. March divulged to Nancy what he proposed to do that evening.

"I have a hunch that fellow Riggin is going to come back here tonight. Well, he'll be my prisoner before he knows what's happening."

"You mean you'll notify the police?"

"Indeed not. This old soldier is going to capture the thief alone!"

Nancy was aghast, and started to object.

"Nothing would please me more than to get my hands on the fellow who stole Fipp's work!" Mr. March insisted.

Nancy could not persuade him to change his mind. She offered to accompany him, but he would not let her.

"You said you wanted to think things out," Mr. March reminded her. "Maybe an idea will come to you and you'll go back to the old attic and search for the rest of my son's music."

"At least, let's arrange a signal," Nancy pleaded. "Couldn't you imitate some kind of an animal sound to let me know if the man shows up?"

Mr. March grinned. "I can try hooting like an owl."

"Good! I'll listen for it."

Saying he would post himself near the old servants' quarters, Mr. March went outdoors quietly. Nancy had some misgivings about his going, but said nothing.

She put Susan to bed, then came downstairs. Effie soon finished her work and retired. The young detective was left alone.

For an hour Nancy sat in the living room, thinking. She reviewed the various angles of the two strange cases in which she and her father had become involved.

"The hardest work is yet to come," she mused, "and that will be to go into court and prove that the two Mr. Dights are guilty. They've both stolen something, but how different the two products are!"

Realizing it would cost Mr. March a great deal of money to carry out his plan of prosecuting the plagiarist, Nancy could not help but wish that there were some way to locate more of Fipp's music. Her thoughts turned suddenly to the piano-desk.

"Why, there may be another secret drawer in it!" she concluded suddenly.

Excited, Nancy jumped up and started for the attic, carrying a candle. As she reached the third floor a clock chimed.

She smiled. "The witching hour of midnight! And I hope all's well," she quoted.

Nancy started her new investigation of the piano-desk. The utter stillness and the close atmosphere had a depressing effect upon her. She began to breathe more quickly as first one sound, then another made her uneasy.

"They seem so far away," she thought. "I wonder if I would hear Mr. March if he should call."

For a long moment Nancy stood still, hesitant to go on with her work. Maybe she ought to run downstairs to be near the elderly man if he needed her.

"I'll hurry with my search," she decided.

Nancy pressed first one area, then another on the left-hand side of the old piece of furniture. No drawer came out. She tried again and again, then switched to the right-hand side. At last her efforts were rewarded.

Slowly a shallow tray moved out from the middle of the old piano-desk. It was filled with papers.

Nancy's pulse was beating wildly, but she forced herself to be calm. She carried the tray to the table, then took out several scrolls and folded papers.

Nancy scanned them hastily. As she had hoped, they were all musical compositions. The name Philip March Jr. was signed in a bold scrawl at the top of each song!

"These have never been published!" Nancy thought elatedly. "That thief didn't find them!"

Her imagination was spinning as she hummed one lovely air after another and realized what hits they would make. Nancy could picture the shabby old mansion restored to its former grandeur. Little Susan would be getting a fine education. Mr. March . . .

Nancy was so absorbed in her thoughts she failed to notice that the piano-desk was moving slowly and silently across the floor. It stopped. Then noiselessly a man raised himself through a hole. He began to smile.

"So she found them for me!" he gloated.

Nancy, unaware that her every move was being watched, rolled up the manuscripts. As she started to pick up the candle, the young sleuth became aware of a sound behind her!

Nancy froze to the spot. The stealthy intruder confronted her. Before she could scream, he grabbed her in a powerful grip and put one hand over her mouth.

"Bushy Trott!" she gurgled behind his fat fingers.

"Mr. Riggin Trott, if you please!" he corrected her with a sneer. "I see you remember me. Well, I remember *you*. Tried to spy on me at the Dight factory, didn't you? Well, that didn't get you anywhere!"

Nancy fought to escape from the man, but his clutch was like an iron vise. He whipped out a handkerchief and stuffed it into her mouth. Deftly he produced two pieces of rope from his pocket.

"Always carry these for emergencies," he announced with a low chuckle. "Use them for people who don't mind their own business. I threw a stone at old man March at your house to scare you from coming here. But I'm glad you came."

Nancy kicked at the man's shins, and he winced with pain.

"Goin' to fight, eh? I'll fix that," he sneered.

Having tied Nancy's hands behind her, Trott now pushed the young detective down and bound her ankles. She fought desperately, but it was useless. When he had her completely at his mercy, he grinned evilly.

"Many thanks for solving the baffling mystery!" he said. "For a long while I've been trying to learn where the rest of the March music was hidden. Now I'll relieve you of your precious bundle."

He picked up the manuscripts, which had fallen to the floor in the scuffle, and put them under one arm. Then he reached into a pocket.

"I'm sorry to leave you like this," he said sardonically, "but I trust that this little creature will fix you so you'll remember nothing of this episode."

Nancy, squirming and twisting, did not understand what the man meant. He removed a bottle from his pocket.

"You wonder what this is?" he jested cruelly. "A black widow, my dear detective. Oh, you shudder? Then you know what it will do to you!"

CHAPTER XIX

Deadly Darkness

Bushy Trott's eyes gleamed like a maniac's as he laid the spider on a corner of the piano-desk. At once it started to crawl toward the floor and he gave a low laugh of satisfaction.

Nancy rolled herself sideways to get out of its path. Her eyes focused for a second on the three steps to the attic.

"If only I could pull myself up them, I might be able to escape!"

"Don't expect any help from the old man," Trott said with a look of satisfaction. "March is sound asleep in the garden, and he won't wake up for a long, long time!"

The man chuckled, pleased with his accomplishment. Nancy's heart nearly stopped beating. What had he done to Mr. March?

"Now just to be sure nobody else comes here,"

Trott continued, "I'll fix that attic door so it can't be opened."

Nancy's heart sank as he moved to the opening through which she had hoped to escape. He swung the battered door shut, then rearranged the long, wooden bar which she and Mr. March had broken down.

Thoroughly enjoying himself, Bushy Trott looked around. Seeing the spider, he scooped it up in the bottle and shook it, "Just to liven the thing up a bit," he said. Once more the man held it above the piano-desk. The black widow crawled out and dropped onto the yellowed keys of the instrument.

"I always carry one of these with me in case of need," Trott explained. "Well, good night, young lady!" He grinned at Nancy. "And good-by. Good-by forever."

To her horror, he picked up the candle and retreated to the opening in the floor which Nancy guessed led to the old servants' quarters. She struggled desperately to free herself.

"You can't escape," Trott taunted her. "The black widow may not come quickly, but she'll finally find you."

The man held the candle in the direction of the piano-desk. Nancy saw the spider climbing slowly down one leg of the instrument. It was not a dozen feet away from her.

"Sweet dreams!" whispered Trott, blowing out the candle.

He took a flashlight from his pocket, turned it on, then lowered himself into the opening. Before disappearing he pulled the piano-desk over the hole.

The old attic was in complete darkness. Nancy knew the black widow was coming closer to her, but she had no idea which way to roll to avoid its deadly bite.

Nancy expected the poisonous spider to strike any moment. Then a thought came to her. Perhaps if she lay very still, the spider might decide she was not going to harm it and leave her alone.

Suddenly Nancy's anger at Trott's vile deed took possession of her. No one but herself could testify that he had stolen Fipp March's music, and that he carried deadly black widows to use on anyone who might stand in his way.

"I must get out of here!" Nancy told herself over and over again. "That terrible man must be arrested at once."

She could not scream, nor could she loosen her bonds. Nancy found, however, that she was able to raise both her feet and thump them hard on the floor. Would the sounds carry to Effie's room? And if they did, would the timid maid come upstairs, break down the door, and venture into the secret room?

"I believe she'd do that if she thought I was in danger," Nancy reassured herself.

She rolled across the floor until reaching the steps to the main attic. Then she pounded on them with all her might. After waiting several minutes and getting no response, Nancy gave up hope of rescue from this source.

"If I could only move the piano-desk and get down that hole!" she thought. "There must be a stairway." Then Nancy realized that in the pitch blackness she would probably fall and be badly injured.

Suddenly Nancy heard her name called. The sound was far away. Her heart sank. But in a moment hurrying footsteps came from somewhere.

"Nancy! Nancy!" a male voice called out.

"Oh, I hope I'm not imagining things," she thought.

"Nancy! Where are you?" a girl shouted.

Now she could hear jumbled voices in the big attic. Again her name was called.

Nancy thumped with all her strength. The next instant a body crashed against the door, and it burst open. A flashlight shone in her eyes.

"Thank goodness you're safe!" were the words Nancy heard. She could hardly believe her good fortune. The speaker was Ned Nickerson.

Bess, George, and Effie crowded into the room

after him. But Ned took complete charge of the situation.

Springing forward, he jerked the gag from Nancy's mouth. Then he cut her bonds with his pocketknife and helped the girl to her feet.

"Nancy, if anything had happened to you— Who did this?" he demanded gruffly.

"Bushy Trott. Oh, Ned—"

Her arm shaking, she pointed to the floor. The black widow was less than two feet away!

As Effie let out a scream, Ned crushed the spider with his foot. The others murmured in relief.

"Have any of you seen Mr. March?" Nancy asked quickly.

The others gazed at her, perplexed.

"Isn't he in bed?" Effie asked.

Nancy told them of Bushy Trott's sinister words. Like a shot George dashed down the stairs of the old attic on her way to the garden. Bess and Effie followed.

Nancy started after them, but Ned held her back. "Are you really all right?" he asked in deep concern.

"Yes, Ned." She smiled at him. "I was pretty scared for a while, I admit, but I'm okay now. Really."

"Boy, you sure gave me a scare!" Ned said.

Together they went downstairs quickly and outdoors.

"By the old servants' quarters," Nancy called to the girls.

She led the way as Ned held the flashlight. Under a lilac bush they found the crumpled form of Mr. March. Effie let out a frightened moan.

"Is he—is he—?"

Ned pulled the still figure from beneath the bush. Nancy felt the elderly man's pulse.

"He's alive," she said. "But the shock may prove to be too much for him."

They carried Mr. March into the house. Under their kindly ministrations, he quickly regained consciousness. Nancy had warned the others not to tell him what had happened in the secret room. Presently he went upstairs to rest.

"I have to go to River Heights right away," said Nancy. "Effie, I can't explain now, but you'll be all right here alone. That shadowy figure will never come back."

"Thank goodness!" said the maid. "You and your friends go right along, and I'll take good care of Mr. March."

"Where are you going?" George asked.

"To Mr. Dight. I know he has the address of Bushy Trott!"

Explanations were in order on both sides. Nancy suggested they tell their stories while riding along. When they went outside, the young people saw a car turn into the driveway of Pleas-

ant Hedges. The man at the wheel proved to be
Mr. Drew.

"What luck!" Nancy cried out. "Oh, Dad, I'm
so glad to see you," she said hurriedly as he
stopped at the door. "Can you go to Mr. Dight's
house with us right away?"

"Sure can," he replied. "But what's up? More
clues?"

"It was Bushy Trott who was stealing Fipp
March's music! And he got away with the rest of
it tonight! We must find out his address from
Lawrence Dight and then notify the police!"

"Hop into my car, everybody!" Carson Drew
called out.

Nancy gave her father and her friends the story
of her evening's adventure in detail. At Nancy's
recital of her experience being tied up in the
dark with a black widow spider, Mr. Drew was
shocked.

"You shouldn't take such chances," he told his
daughter. "Bravery is one thing, but dealing with
a man like Trott—"

Nancy said, "How could I have guessed there
was a trap door under the piano-desk? Anyway,
it's fortunate that my friends rescued me," she
added cheerfully.

"It was just luck that we did," Ned explained.
"Tonight when I came to River Heights, even
though it was getting late, I wanted to see you.

Mrs. Gruen told me where you were, and I got Bess and George to show me the way out here."

By this time Mr. Drew had reached River Heights. Bess thought that she and George ought to go home, and were driven to their respective houses.

"If you and your father have a job to do," said Ned, "perhaps I should go too."

"Oh please stay!" Nancy urged.

Mr. Drew added, "I believe we'll need an extra man before the night's over! One with good strong muscles!"

CHAPTER XX

Plotter Nabbed

WHEN Mr. Drew drove up to the Dight home, it was in darkness. Nevertheless he pounded on the front door. Finally Mr. Dight came to let them in.

"What's the meaning of this call in the middle of the night?" he demanded angrily.

The lawyer did not waste words. He stated that he wanted to prefer charges against Riggin Trott and demanded the man's address.

"I don't even know the fellow," Lawrence Dight blustered. "What do you mean by coming here and waking me up with such a stupid question?"

"Maybe you know him as Bushy Trott," Mr. Drew suggested. "We have proof that he stole a silk-making process from his former employer Mr. Booker. You're using that same formula in your own plant."

"Nonsense!"

"There is no denying it," Mr. Drew declared. "My daughter obtained samples of fluid from two different vats in your laboratory. Tests prove them to be the same content as the Booker mixtures."

Nancy spoke up. "Your employee Trott tonight tried to kill me by tying me up and leaving a black widow spider loose to poison me!"

The information seemed to stun Mr. Dight.

"I knew nothing of that," he insisted in a frightened voice. "We have poisonous spiders at our plant but—"

"There are also other charges against Bushy Trott. Will you give me his address?"

Mr. Dight was shaking. "Yes, I will. I assure you I didn't knowingly use the Booker silk-making process. Nor did I suspect that Trott was trying to make trouble for your daughter. I'm glad nothing happened to her."

Lawrence Dight went quickly to a desk and wrote down Trott's home address.

"To tell the truth, I thought for a time Nancy Drew was trying to steal *our* plant formula," he told the callers. "We purchased the new silk-making process from Trott recently at a high price."

Mr. Dight sighed and did not speak for several seconds.

Finally he went on, "I've kept the silk-making

process at the factory a secret, because I was afraid all the workmen in the place might leave if they knew there were poisonous spiders around."

"The secret you guard so carefully already belongs to my client Mr. Booker," replied Carson Drew. "The only difference is that your man uses poisonous spiders. From what happened tonight, I judge he has a mania for the deadly things."

Mr. Dight looked incredulous. "You mean to say Bushy Trott sold me a process which he neither owned nor controlled?"

"Exactly."

"Then I've been tricked!" shouted the factory owner. "I'll telephone the police immediately and have the man arrested."

Within ten minutes a patrol car was speeding to the Trott home. Mr. Drew, Nancy, and Ned followed in the lawyer's automobile. They arrived in time to see Trott being led from the house by two policemen. He turned deathly white when he saw Nancy.

"You!" he cried unbelievingly. "How? Where did you come from?"

"Is this the man?" one of the officers asked her, seeking a positive identification.

"Yes," she replied. "I believe his right name is Riggin Trott."

The following day Nancy and her father asked the police if they might speak to the prisoner.

Police supplied the information that Trott was an ex-convict. Though he was a clever chemist, after prison he had worked as a chauffeur for Horace Dight, the cousin of Diane's father.

"Well, that explains a number of things!" cried Nancy.

Trott talked willingly. Nancy asked, "You sold Philip March's music manuscripts to Horace Dight, didn't you?"

Trott nodded. He said that Dight, always struggling to compose a song which would sell, was hard-pressed financially. One day Trott had slyly suggested to his employer that he knew where salable songs might be obtained.

"I didn't tell him where, though."

As it developed, Trott had known Fipp March in the army, and made it a point to win his confidence, planning to rob the March mansion eventually.

"But he didn't tell me exactly where he had hidden the music," the prisoner went on.

After Trott got out of the service, he soon landed in jail. By the time he reached the March mansion a few years later the place seemed hardly worth looting. When he took employment with Horace Dight, Trott remembered that Fipp had often played his numerous unpublished compositions. The thief was determined to search for them. One day when the family was out of town

Trott had explored the main attic. He had discovered the crude door covered by the heavy wardrobe and had investigated the second room. He had found a song which Fipp had left on the piano-desk. He had sold it to Horace Dight, who had asked for more immediately.

"Next I looked for a stairway from the second attic," Trott said. "Fipp had talked a lot about his childhood in the old house. Once when he was playing in the servants' section he discovered a door which didn't look like a door. It opened onto a narrow stairway leading up toward the section of attic above the servants' quarters. I found the hole in the floor and went down. Later I put the piano-desk over it."

Trott said that after his discovery he had secretly entered the March house by this means. He had terrified Effie, and his footsteps had echoed weirdly through the old mansion. In vain the man had searched for the missing music. To his surprise the drawer below the piano keys had opened, revealing two songs. It was then that Trott had dropped the telltale note that Nancy had found.

He turned the musical compositions over to Horace Dight, who had them published under the names of Ben Banks and Harry Hall. The songs quickly became popular. Bushy Trott determined to find all of Fipp's creations.

Trott was convinced that the music must be hidden somewhere in the piano-desk. As he continued to search, he became alarmed, thinking that he might be caught, because Nancy and her friends came with increasing frequency to the attic.

Cunningly Trott decided to frighten everyone away. He bored a hole through the secret door back of the wardrobe and also through the wardrobe itself. Then he released a deadly black widow spider from its bottle. It had later crawled through the tiny opening and bitten Effie.

"I was desperate," Trott said.

Nancy asked, "What about Horace Dight?"

Nancy learned that he was so pleased by the success of the stolen songs that he urged Trott to find other compositions for him. The publisher had never suspected anything illegal and first found out that his client was not the composer when he talked with Nancy at the March mansion.

"The men had words," Trott revealed, "and there were threats on both sides. But finally Mr. Jenner agreed to keep the matter a secret, since he was making money on the musical hits."

Horace Dight, now in Trott's clutches, aided the man in various other crimes. He sent him to his gullible cousin, Lawrence Dight, and planned to profit handsomely from the sale of the stolen silk-making process.

Due to the astuteness of Nancy and her father, both Horace Dight and Riggin Trott would now be out of circulation for some time. Diane's father, who knew nothing of his cousin's criminal activities, had agreed to pay royalties to Mr. Booker for the use of his formula. The two men were also considering a company merger which would be equitable to both.

One day as Nancy was discussing the forthcoming dance at Emerson College with Bess and George, a parcel arrived for her from the Booker factory.

"Would you like to see what I'm going to wear to the Emerson dance?" she asked Bess and George, her eyes sparkling. "Come up to my room and we'll open this."

The three girls went upstairs. From the box Nancy brought out a pale-yellow evening dress, soft and beautiful in texture.

"Oh!" Bess cried. "I never saw anything lovelier. Where did you get it?"

"Mr. Booker sent it to me. He's a client of Dad's." Nancy wished she might tell her friends more, but she had promised the manufacturer she would not divulge his secret.

"I'll bet you helped your dad on a case," George said wisely, "and this is your reward."

"You're right," Nancy admitted.

Bess chuckled. "Ask your father if he has a mystery for me to solve with the same reward!"

The girls laughed, then Nancy said, "Anyway, the next mystery I have I'll share with you."

True to her word, Bess and George were invited to join Nancy in solving another perplexing case, *The Clue in the Crumbling Wall.*

A couple of days later Mr. Drew said to his daughter, "You've made two firm friends. I just stopped in to call on Mr. March and Susan. Mr. Jenner has agreed to compensate them for Fipp's stolen songs, and my friend Hank Hawkins is going to publish all the other compositions. The Marches are delighted and you should hear all the wonderful things they had to say about you!"

"I'm glad to have helped them." Nancy smiled modestly. "And it was exciting to hunt for clues in the spooky old attic."

"Nevertheless it took courage," her father replied. "If you hadn't had it, you never would have discovered the attic's secrets."

Match Wits with The Hardy Boys®!

Collect the Complete
Hardy Boys Mystery Stories®
by Franklin W. Dixon

The Hardy Boys Back-to-Back

Celebrate over 70 Years with the World's Greatest Super Sleuth

Match Wits with Super Sleuth Nancy Drew!

Collect the Complete
Nancy Drew Mystery Stories®
by Carolyn Keene

Celebrate over 70 years with the World's Best Detective!